Vanilla Whip and Murder

Holly Holmes Cozy Culinary Mystery – book 3

K.E. O'Connor

K.E. O'Connor Books

VANILLA WHIP AND MURDER

ISBN: 978-1-9163573-2-7

Written by K.E. O'Connor

Edited by Amy Hart

Cover design by Stunning Book Covers

Beta read by my wonderful early review team. You're all amazing.

Chapter 1

"One more big push and we can freewheel down the next hill, Meatball."

"Woof woof." My adorable corgi cross poked his tongue out, and his stubby tail wagged as the wind blew his ears back.

I sucked in a deep breath as the last hill in Audley St. Mary confronted me. I was tired from a morning of cake deliveries around the pretty village. It seemed like everyone couldn't get enough of the delicious treats we made at Audley Castle.

A car rumbled up behind me before slowing, and the horn was tooted.

I inched to the edge of the road. It was a narrow lane, so it made it tricky for cars to pass me safely.

The horn tooted again, several times.

I lifted my right hand off the handlebar and gestured for them to drive around me.

The car maneuvered next to me and the window slid down. Cecilia Montgomery smiled at me. "Busy day, Holly?"

"It's always busy at the castle, Cecilia. How's the dress shop going?"

1

"I can't complain. I had Princess Alice in just last week. She bought half of my stock."

"She does love to shop," I said.

"You won't hear me complaining about that. Have a nice day." Cecilia tooted her horn again before zooming off in her sporty black two-seater. The couture business was clearly doing well for her.

I gave Meatball a quick tickle under his furry brown chin before digging in and making it to the crest of the hill, trying hard not to wish for a car just like Cecilia's. Cars cost money, and my work bike was a free and easy way to keep fit.

And with all the cycling I'd done today on my delivery round, I more than deserved the strawberry cream pie nestled in the bike basket. It was tucked in a box to keep it away from Meatball.

At my last delivery, Mr. Johnson had not only given me a tip but also one of my own cakes. I was planning on putting my feet up for five minutes and enjoying it with a big mug of tea before I got on with the baking that needed doing in the Audley Castle kitchen.

Loud dance music pounded from a vehicle approaching behind me at speed. I hugged the curb and concentrated on keeping the wheels of the bike straight to give the vehicle enough room to pass me.

A horn blasted and there was a screech of tires. My back wheel was bumped.

I gasped and clutched the handlebars. You have got to be kidding me? Someone was trying to run me off the road.

"Woof!" Meatball's eyes narrowed, and he growled.

"It's okay. It's just someone who needs to go back to driver's school."

My back wheel was nudged again. That time, it was deliberate.

"Get off the road, you idiot!" A shiny red sports car screeched around me, the music blaring and the windows down. There was a flash of long dark hair, and then it was gone.

"I'm the idiot?" I tried to get control of the bike, but the front wheel hit a hole in the road, and I lurched sideways.

I reached out and caught Meatball to keep him safe as the bike pitched over.

I crashed to the ground, Meatball protected by my arms forming a shield around him. A pedal whacked my shin as I hit the muddy ground with a bone jarring thump.

I blinked several times, my heart thundering, and my breath coming out in panicked gasps. "That crazy driver could have killed us."

Meatball licked the palm of my hand and whined.

"Are you okay, boy?" I used my free hand to lift the heavy frame of the bike off me and winced as I pulled my leg out from underneath it. Nothing felt broken, but there was a gash on my shin.

Once I was free from under the bike, I scooped Meatball up and checked him over. As usual, he wore his cycling helmet and had been cushioned from the fall by my arms and his blanket.

I cuddled him to me as I twisted my ankles in different directions. Nothing felt strained, but the cuts on my legs stung and the skin felt hot.

I groaned as I checked the bike. The front wheel had buckled when I'd hit the hole.

This wouldn't be the first time I'd damaged the castle's delivery bike. My boss, Chef Heston, would be less than impressed. He'd no doubt take the repairs for the bike out of my wages. But this wasn't my fault. That terrible driver had almost killed me, and he hadn't even slowed down to make sure I was okay. He must have seen me fall off the bike.

A driver in a sleek soft top black Audi cruised past. The brake lights flashed on before the car reversed and stopped beside me. The passenger side window slid down.

A guy with brilliant blue eyes and a hint of dark stubble on his chin leaned over and peered down at me. He looked vaguely familiar. "What are you doing down there?"

"Thanking my lucky stars that I wasn't killed by some idiot in a sports car who doesn't know how to drive," I said. "He just ran me off the road. He hit my bike with his car, twice. He didn't even stop after I fell."

The guy rested a hand on the open window shelf, and I saw a flash of green and black tattoo swirls lacing up his forearm.

I placed Meatball on the ground and stood slowly, my left leg protesting as I did so.

"Did you get his license plate?" the guy asked. "You can always report him to the police."

"No, I was too busy trying not to fall off my bike."

"You didn't do a good job of that." A smirk crossed his face.

"You think!" I wasn't usually this sharp with people, but my heart still raced from the close call. "Hey, are you going to Audley Castle? I won't be able to ride my bike back. I could do with a lift."

He was silent for a long second. "The castle? Why are you going there?"

"I work there," I said.

"Are you a cleaner or something?"

"No! What makes you say that?"

"I definitely didn't figure you for a member of the Audley family." He chuckled as his gaze ran over me.

"Maybe I decided not to wear my tiara today when I came out on a ride. For all you know, you could be speaking to Princess Alice Audley."

He tipped his head back and roared with laughter. "You're not her. I've seen plenty of pictures of Princess Alice. You're the complete opposite of her. She's blonde, curvy, and cute. You're ..." He waved a hand at me.

I bristled at his implied insult. I may not have curves to die for, but I was happy with the way I looked. "Even so, I could be a cousin or a relative of the family."

"But are you?"

I huffed out a breath. "No! But I am in need of help after almost being killed. Surely you can fit my bike in the back of your car. Audley Castle isn't far from here."

He checked his watch and shook his head. "No can do. I'm late for an appointment. Besides, I'm not going that way. Nothing's broken, is it?"

"That's hardly the point. I could be in shock. I may have a concussion. I'm a damsel in distress."

"You're also a damsel wearing an enormous cycling helmet who's quite happy to stand here and argue with me. That suggests your head is fine. You can find your own way to the castle." He roared the engine as the window slid up, and he zoomed off.

My mouth dropped open. So much for chivalry.

Meatball whined, and I turned to see him sniffing the squashed cake box underneath the bike.

I gently eased the bike off the box. It was squashed flat. My delicious treat was ruined, along with the rest of my day, all thanks to my encounter with unhelpful men driving cars that probably cost ten years of my salary.

I righted the bike and checked the front wheel. It was too crooked to ride.

I reached into my back pocket where my phone usually was. Just perfect. I must have left it back in my apartment. I'd been running late that morning, and it had been a mad dash to get to the kitchen in time.

"It looks like we have to help ourselves, Meatball." I scooped him up, kissed him on the head, and placed him back in the basket. "At least I have you. You'll never let me down."

"Woof woof." He rested his front paws on the edge of the basket as I slowly pushed the damaged bike toward the castle. It was only about a mile away, but with my sore leg, it felt a lot farther.

"If I ever see that idiot driver again, we're having words. Why is it always the people who drive the posh sports cars who have terrible manners and are awful drivers?" That wasn't always true, but I was too angry to be rational. "If I was in charge, I'd make anyone who drove a sports car have extra driving lessons so they knew how to handle something so powerful."

"Woof woof." Meatball heartily agreed as he surveyed the beautiful countryside I limped past.

At least the weather was on our side. It was a glorious sunny day, and white clouds scudded across a brilliant blue sky. Birds sung in the treetops, and by the time I'd reached the gates of Audley Castle, my bad mood had faded. Despite losing my cake, twisting my bike wheel, and having a scratched-up leg, there was always something positive to focus upon.

"Good gracious, what happened to you?" Lord Rupert Audley raced toward me as I walked along the gravel driveway toward the entrance to the kitchen.

"I met someone who doesn't know how to drive." I happily let him take the bike off me.

Rupert pushed his messy blond hair out of his eyes, and his gaze ran over me. "You haven't been hurt, have you?"

"A few cuts on my leg, but nothing serious," I said. "The bike definitely came off worse."

"Let's get this bike back to the shed and get you patched up," he said. "Do you need to see the doctor? You didn't hit your head?"

I rapped my knuckles on my helmet. "No. I was shocked when it happened, but I'll be fine."

"Your pants are torn," Rupert said. "And you've cut your knee."

"The bike fell on me, and I hit some stones when I landed," I said. "It's just a surface wound."

"You should take the rest of the day off," he said. "I can look after you. It'll be my pleasure to make sure the finest baker in the castle is safe and well. We don't want you out of action and depriving the world of your desserts."

I grinned. After my encounter with two unpleasant men, it was nice to meet a genuinely sweet person. Rupert always had a way of making me feel better.

"There's no need. And I've still got work to do in the kitchen before I can finish for the day."

"I'm sure Chef Heston won't mind if you need the afternoon off," he said. "Maybe I could suggest it to him."

"No! Chef Heston thinks I curry favor with you so I don't have to work so hard."

"I don't believe you'd ever do that. I've never seen anyone work as hard as you do," Rupert said.

I did work hard, but that was because I loved what I did. I always got such satisfaction from making delicious treats and cakes to sell to people. I felt lucky to work in Audley Castle and be surrounded by all this finery every day.

A loud squeal pierced my ears, and I winced as I stepped back.

A woman with long blonde hair raced toward Rupert and engulfed him in an enormous hug. "I've been wondering where you were." She planted a kiss on his cheek.

From her high forehead, bright blue eyes, and heart-shaped face, she had to be one of the Duke and Duchess's daughters.

"Caroline! I didn't know you'd arrived." Rupert scooped Meatball out and placed him on the ground before setting the bike down and hugging her back. "You look as striking as ever."

"And you look as messy as ever." She ruffled his hair. "Are you sure there aren't birds nesting up there?"

He chuckled as he glanced at me. His gaze went over Caroline's shoulder to the woman standing just behind her. She was shorter and thinner and her hair was pale brown.

"Henrietta, I'm glad you could make it," he said.

She nodded and lifted her cheek as he went over to kiss her. "I didn't have much choice."

"Don't be a spoilsport," Caroline said. "Who doesn't love a party?"

Henrietta raised her hand.

Caroline tutted and shook her head. "You're such a party pooper."

"I haven't seen you at the castle for such a long time," Rupert said.

"I've been too busy traveling to visit," Caroline said.

"More like wasting her trust fund," Henrietta muttered.

I felt the urge to make a discreet exit. When I was around Rupert and Alice, it was easy to forget that they were part of an ancient noble family, with royal connections. They always made me feel so welcome and at ease.

Rupert turned to me and extended a hand, as if sensing my discomfort. "This is Holly Holmes. She's the most exquisite baker you will ever discover. She works in our kitchens. We were extremely lucky to get her."

I nodded at both women. "It's nice to meet you."

"These are my cousins, Caroline and Henrietta Audley," Rupert said.

Just as I'd figured, two of the Duke and Duchess's daughters. They had four daughters, Caroline, Henrietta,

Diana, and Mary.

"I look forward to trying your cakes." Caroline tilted her head. "Actually, I've heard about them before. Rupert's always going on about the delicious treats he gets from the kitchen. I always get hungry when he talks about them. Is that your work?"

"Sometimes," I said. "Desserts are my speciality."

"She really is excellent," Rupert said.

"If that's the case, I shall steal her for our kitchen," Caroline said. "Rupert always lets me have whatever I want."

"Holly will never leave us," Rupert said, shooting me a shy look. "I expect you're involved with the anniversary party food. It won't be the same without your tempting treats."

I shook my head. "Chef Heston is leading on that, and there's an outside team coming in to make the preparations."

"Of course. Only the best for our sister." Caroline rolled her eyes. "Honestly, the amount of money they spent on that wedding; now they're doing it all again simply for a boring anniversary."

"They've been married five years," Rupert said. "That's something to celebrate."

Caroline sighed. "I guess so. Diana even had the cheek to issue a gift list. She's not getting anything from me. Not until she returns my favorite cashmere that she borrowed and never gave back. That can be her gift. Although I'm not sure it will suit her husband."

"It should be a fun party," Rupert said. "It's nice to get everyone back together."

"Not everybody's here," Henrietta said quietly, her gaze on the ground.

"Yes! Silly Mary made some excuse about traveling. She sent her apologies," Caroline said. "I'm glad she's not here. My sister's sour face would spoil the party. And if she did come, she'd only say something rude and upset everyone."

Rupert chuckled and rubbed the back of his neck. "She's not that bad. Mary simply likes to speak her mind."

"She likes saying outrageous things to annoy people and cause a scandal," Caroline said. "I don't know why she can't just let her hair down and enjoy herself."

"Like you, you mean," Henrietta said. "Your hair is always down."

Caroline jabbed a finger at her. "Don't you start. You're not much better than Mary. I bet you bring a book to the party. If I see you sneaking out to the library, I'm dragging you back and forcing you to dance. And I'm going to make sure you wear something nice."

"I always wear nice things." Henrietta smoothed her hands down her plain navy, knee-length dress.

"I'm going to do your hair and makeup and make you wear something low-cut. This is a proper party," Caroline said.

Henrietta simply shook her head and looked toward the castle.

"We must go." Caroline pressed another kiss to Rupert's cheek. "I need to catch up with Mommy and Daddy and tell them all my news. And if I have to sort out Henrietta's terrible hair, I need all the time I can get. Maybe we should dye it."

"You're not touching my hair," Henrietta said.

"We'll see about that." Caroline grabbed Henrietta's arm.

"I'll see you both later for dinner," Rupert said.

"Of course. We've got so much to catch up on, and I want to hear everything about the party plans. I can't wait." Caroline hurried away with Henrietta.

Rupert returned to my side, picked up the bike, and we walked over to the sheds. "That's the first time you've met my cousins, isn't it?"

I nodded. "I can see the family resemblance."

"They're great fun," he said. "As you may have noticed, Caroline's the life and soul of the party. Henrietta, not so much, but I like her quiet ways."

"They both seem very nice," I said. I stopped dead and my eyes widened. Parked around the side of the castle was the red sports car that had run me off the road.

"Is something wrong?" Rupert asked.

Meatball growled at the car before running over to sniff it.

"Who does that car belong to?" I asked.

"Oh! I think that's Blaine's car. He's a friend of Percy's, Diana's husband. I suspect he'll be coming to the party tomorrow night. He must have gotten here early."

My gaze narrowed, and I pressed my lips together. So, the idiot who had almost killed me was going to be at this party. If I had a mind to, I might doctor his food as revenge. Maybe some chocolate laxatives in his dessert would teach him a lesson.

I shook my head. I wasn't that vindictive, but it was tempting.

"You don't like the car?" Rupert asked when I didn't respond.

"Oh! Sorry, my mind was elsewhere. It's a great car. A bit flashy for my taste, though." I gave it one more glare, giving a nod of satisfaction when Meatball peed up a wheel.

"Are you sure you're okay to work?" Rupert placed the damaged bike in the shed and shut the door.

"Of course. It takes a lot to keep me out of the kitchen. I must go. Thanks for helping me with the bike." We said our goodbyes, and I limped away.

I settled Meatball into his kennel outside the kitchen and removed his helmet, taking mine off as well, before heading into the kitchen.

I shrugged off my jacket, hung up the cycling helmets, and walked through to wash up before beginning a relaxing afternoon of baking.

My jaw dropped, and I stopped walking.

Standing in the center of the kitchen, with a smug look on his face, was the tattooed man who'd refused to help me.

Chapter 2

"Hey, you!" I stomped over to the man standing in the kitchen, looking like he owned the place, and jabbed a finger at him. "You told me you weren't coming to the castle. You said you were running late for an appointment and couldn't help me after my accident."

The man towered over me, a sly smile creeping across his face. "Oh, that's right. You're the serving girl who was in the ditch when I drove past."

"First off, I'm not a serving girl, I'm a baker in this kitchen, and an extremely good one. And second, I was in that ditch because I was almost run over. I was injured, and you didn't help me. Why lie?"

He shrugged. "I didn't want to get my car dirty with your damaged bike. I've just had it detailed. Plus, you had mud and blood all over your clothes. You still do. You shouldn't be in the kitchen in that state."

"I was injured! I don't normally look like this."

"And did I spot some hairy mutt with you? That thing was definitely not getting in my car."

I glared at him. "You're a real piece of work. Any decent person would have offered to help."

"Maybe I'm not a decent person."

"What are you even doing in this kitchen? You don't work here."

"What's going on?" Chef Heston strode over. "Lorcan, is there a problem?"

The guy's gaze slid my way. "There may be. Does she really work in your kitchen?"

Chef Heston glared at me before nodding. "She does. This is Holly Holmes. Why do you ask?"

"I'm not sure she's a good influence. Perhaps she shouldn't be around while I'm working in here."

"You're … working in this kitchen?" I shook my head. "Please don't tell me you've taken a job here."

Chef Heston grabbed my arm and marched me away. "Of course he hasn't. Don't you know who that is?"

"He's a selfish, rude man who didn't help me when I fell off my bike. Or should I say, I was driven into a ditch by someone."

Chef Heston sucked air through his teeth. "Did you damage the bike again?"

"The bike! Don't worry about asking if I'm okay."

His gaze ran over me. "You seem fine. Holly, that's Lorcan Blaze."

My head whipped round to stare at Lorcan. Of course, I recognized him now. He was the go-to guy when it came to celebrity cakes. I'd seen his picture in numerous magazines.

"What's he doing here?" I asked.

"He's been brought in to provide the cake for the anniversary party. We should be privileged that he's using our kitchen."

My gaze slid Lorcan's way again. He was still smirking, probably thrilled that I was getting reprimanded. I didn't feel privileged by him being here. "Lorcan should have helped me after I'd fallen off my bike."

"I'm sure he had bigger things on his mind than helping you after your little tumble."

"It was more than a little—"

"Enough!" Chef Heston lifted a finger. "You will get along with Lorcan while he's working in this kitchen. It's important the party goes without a hitch."

"How about I simply stay out of his way, so long as he stays out of mine?"

His eyes narrowed. "Don't cause any trouble. Lorcan's a master at what he does. We'll all be able to pick up useful tips from him."

There were so many rude things I wanted to say, but I pressed my lips together and simply nodded. There was no point in getting on the wrong side of Chef Heston. He was fan boying all over Lorcan Blaze, and nothing I said would change his mind.

"I'm glad we understand each other." He dropped his hold on my arm. "Be on your best behavior. And go and get changed before you start work. Lorcan's right, those clothes shouldn't be seen in this kitchen. And you have mud on your cheek."

"Yes, Chef." I glared at Lorcan, and he grinned back as I stomped out of the kitchen and dashed to my apartment. I threw my muddy, torn clothes into the laundry hamper before bathing the cuts on my knee and shin, making sure there were no bits of stone left in the wounds.

After I'd dressed my injuries and put on a clean uniform, I headed back to the kitchen.

My bad mood, which had been fading, returned in an instant. Lorcan had his equipment laid out in the area I liked to bake in. The surface was covered in trays, piping bags, cake decorations, and a huge cake stand stood in the center of the counter.

Before I had a chance to go over and confront him, Chef Heston stood in front of me. "Remember what I said,

Holly. Best behavior."

"But ... but, he's in my space. Where am I supposed to bake the cakes for the café?"

"As you can see, this is a big kitchen with plenty of preparation areas. Go somewhere else for a couple of days. It won't do you any harm."

"But I know where everything is in my area."

His eyes narrowed. "Stop causing me trouble. We've got a lot going on with the upcoming anniversary party. I don't need anything to distract me. There will be hundreds of guests arriving soon."

Before I had a chance to protest any more, the kitchen door opened.

Princess Alice hurried over to me. "I just heard the news about your accident. Are you okay?"

"I'm fine," I muttered.

"And your poor bike. I heard it got all twisted up."

Chef Heston let out an angry sigh. "Holly!"

"Not my fault," I said.

"Rupert said someone ran you off the road," Alice said. "How terrible."

"It was." I felt a tiny bit better now someone was worrying about me.

Alice patted my arm. "You poor thing. While I'm here, have you got any of those cupcakes with your yummy vanilla whip topping? I'm starving. I only had a salad at lunchtime. I've got this dress I'm supposed to wear for the anniversary party, but it's on the tight side. Do you think I could lose five pounds in twenty-four hours?"

So much for her wanting to check I was okay. Alice just wanted cake. "Probably not if you eat my vanilla whip cupcakes."

Lorcan strolled over and his gaze ran over Alice. His smile turned predatory.

I stepped in front of her. I didn't want him getting anywhere near someone as sweet as Alice.

Chef Heston moved me to one side. "Lorcan Blaze, I'd like you to meet Princess Alice Audley."

"Charmed, I'm sure." Lorcan bowed, grabbed Alice's hand, and kissed the back of it.

"Goodness! You're very forward." Alice pressed her other hand to her chest as she giggled.

I rolled my eyes and tutted.

Lorcan straightened and glared at me. "Since I've arrived, several people have said that you're the one to watch around here. You reckon you're a hotshot in the kitchen."

"And they'd be right," I said. There was no way I was letting Lorcan intimidate me.

"Holly's the very best baker," Alice said. "She makes the most wonderful cakes. They're like beautiful works of art. And they taste divine. People are always asking which cakes Holly baked. She's an asset to the castle. Don't you think, Chef Heston?"

He grunted. "She does good work when she focuses."

Lorcan's top lip curled. "If you're so good, why don't we have a taste test of your food?"

I gulped. "A taste test? What are you testing my food against?"

"My desserts. We can make this a challenge. The best cake wins."

"Wins what?" I asked.

"You leaving me alone." Lorcan's smile was anything but friendly.

Chef Heston cleared his throat. "My staff don't have time to get involved in that."

Lorcan dismissed his comment with a wave of his hand. "It won't take long. We lay out six different cakes, and I'll try them all. I have a refined palate. I trained in Paris. I can always taste when something is too sweet or cheap ingredients have been used."

"We never use cheap ingredients in the castle kitchen," I said. "Only the best for the family and visitors."

"If that's the case, you won't mind putting your own creations to the test. The Princess seems to think you're something special."

"Holly is very special." Alice patted my arm again. "Challenge accepted."

"Wait! I didn't agree to that," I said.

Alice leaned toward me until her mouth was by my ear. "You'll beat him. Your food is much tastier than anyone else's."

"Then it's agreed." Lorcan clapped his hands together.

"We need to make this fair," Chef Heston said. "You'll know the food you've prepared by sight. There could be a bias, even if it's an unconscious one."

"You're suggesting I'd cheat?" Lorcan scowled at Chef Heston.

"Absolutely not. I can't imagine you'd behave unfairly."

"I could," I muttered.

"Let's make this a blind taste test. Other senses are always heightened when you're unable to see what you're eating. That way, you won't know what you're putting in your mouth," Chef Heston said. "And you both take part. You each sample the desserts on offer and pick your favorites."

"I have no problem with that," Lorcan said. "I'm confident that I'll pick out my food. It'll be the most delicious."

"He's very sure of himself," Alice whispered to me.

He was. But I was also sure about my desserts. Lorcan may have studied in Paris, but I'd spent years perfecting my cakes, cookies, and sweet treats. I'd even run a successful café for a while until a discount coffee chain had moved into the village and stolen my profits. I knew how to make beautiful, delicious desserts that wowed the senses. And I really wanted to wipe that smug smile off Lorcan Blaze's face.

"Select three similar desserts," Chef Heston said. "Something chocolate-based would be good. We have several selections in the café, and I know Holly has recently baked those."

"Brownies, sponge cake, and torte," Lorcan said. "I have all of those in my selection."

"Perfect," Chef Heston said. "We can match that."

The next few minutes were a blur of activity as people hurried around and collected the different chocolate desserts.

A small crowd had gathered to watch the contest by the time everything was laid out.

My stomach tickled with nerves. I had to beat Lorcan. I couldn't let this self-satisfied ego get the better of me. I believed that what goes around comes around. And Lorcan's bad manners toward me were about to bite him in the backside.

Once the desserts had been laid out by Chef Heston, he turned Lorcan and me away from the table. "I'll arrange them in a specific order, but I don't want you to see so there's no unfair advantage."

"I don't need any help in choosing my own desserts," Lorcan said. Still, he turned his back on the table before Chef Heston rearranged the desserts so neither of us could tell which order they were in.

"Tie these cloths around your eyes so you can't see while you eat." Chef Heston handed us each a clean white cloth. "Lorcan, as our guest, you may go first."

I listened to him chewing and muttering to himself as he sampled the treats on offer.

"The first brownie is perfection, the second chocolate sponge option is mine, and the first chocolate torte was made by me. The rest were nothing special," he said. "I can absolutely guarantee that the ones I selected are mine."

The assembled crowd murmured. Was that a good murmur? Had he guessed right? I tried not to panic. I could do this. I knew my puddings.

"Thank you, Lorcan," Chef Heston said. "Holly, now it's your turn." He led me to the table.

A fork was placed in my hand. I took a bite of the first dessert. It had the consistency of a rich chocolate brownie. The chocolate was creamy with a hint of caramel. That had to be mine.

I sampled the second brownie option. It was good, but the chocolate was a bit bitter. That was Lorcan's.

I moved on to my second cake selection. These were the sponge cakes. The first one was great. Light and evenly baked, but there wasn't much flavor to it. You got a hit of chocolate and that was it.

As soon as I tasted the second sponge cake, I knew it was mine. The chocolate lingered and made me want more.

The final options were the chocolate tortes. I bit into the first one. Wow! Amazing flavors. I'd know this anywhere. I'd spent several weeks perfecting this recipe and trying it out in the café. It was our tourists' favorite dessert, and it was always one of the first things to sell out.

I stepped away from the table and lowered my fork.

"What's your verdict, Holly?" Chef Heston sounded eager to hear my answer.

"I agree with Lorcan."

"Hah! You see. My desserts are superior," Lorcan said.

I lowered the blindfold and blinked at Chef Heston.

He glanced from Lorcan to me and cleared his throat. "You both chose Holly's desserts as the favorites."

"What? That's impossible." Lorcan leaned over the table and stared at the desserts. "No, you're mistaken."

"There was no mistake," Chef Heston said. "You picked Holly's desserts."

Lorcan's nostrils flared. "I got my ordering wrong."

"Everyone heard you." Chef Heston gestured to the crowd of onlookers.

"No! I made a mistake."

"You make mistakes?" I couldn't help myself. He'd picked my desserts in a fair contest.

"I … I must have done." Lorcan swiped a hand across his face. "I'd never choose your food over mine."

"Yet you did," Alice said as she gave my shoulder a squeeze.

Chef Heston nodded, and a glimmer of pride filled his gaze. "Congratulations, Holly."

Lorcan scowled. "I didn't mean to pick her desserts. They were simply adequate."

"You're lying!" Alice said. "Holly's desserts are the best."

I caught hold of her arm and shook my head. There was no point in going up against Lorcan. He was a man so full of his own self-importance that he was prepared to lie to prove he was right.

Lorcan glared at me. "If I was your boss, I'd make sure you stuck to serving the food, not baking it. It's very forgettable."

That was it. I'd had enough of his rudeness. I took a step toward him, but Chef Heston intervened and blocked my path. "Lady Philippa's in need of afternoon tea. Holly, take it up to her."

I blinked, the angry flare of red fading as I realized how close I'd come to doing something I'd probably regret. Although squashing one of Lorcan's cakes into his smug face would have been so satisfying.

"Yes! Let's have afternoon tea with Granny," Alice said. "We can take some of these delicious cakes with us. And we must add your vanilla whip cupcakes. I've been dreaming about them ever since I forced down that boring salad at lunch."

Chef Heston led me away from the table and out of earshot of Lorcan. "Take the rest of the afternoon off. I see there's a clash of personalities between you and Lorcan. We don't want to ruffle our superstar's feathers."

"There's only a clash because he's not a nice man," I said.

"He may not be a nice man, but he's here to do a very important job for the Audley family."

"That means he gets to be rude to everyone?" I shook my head. "And what's worse, he lied to us."

Chef Heston's mouth twisted to the side. "The most important thing is that both you and I know he lied. Your desserts were clearly the winner. They always are."

My head jerked back. "You really think so?"

"You know you're excellent at what you do. Don't go fishing for compliments. And if you want to keep your job, take tea and cakes up to Lady Philippa and cool down. I don't want to hear of any more arguments between you and Lorcan."

To do that, I'd have to keep right out of Lorcan's way. Even just looking at him made my blood boil and my fingers clench. "Very well. I can do that."

I collected the tray with the tea things and cakes and hurried out of the kitchen with Alice by my side.

"That cheating chef was good-looking, but I don't think much of his personality," Alice said.

"Same here," I said. "And you haven't experienced the worst of it." I gave her a quick rundown of what happened on the road and how Lorcan refused to help me.

She wrinkled her nose and stuck out her tongue. "What a beast! I won't touch his cake at the party in support of you. In fact, I shall take some of your desserts with me and share them around. If he hadn't been invited to the castle to cater for Diana and Percy's wedding anniversary, I'd insist he leave."

"I wish you could. Meeting him has spoiled my day."

"Here, have this. It will cheer you up." Alice jammed a cupcake into my mouth. "Now, let's go and see Granny and her ghosts."

Chapter 3

Alice strode ahead of me toward Lady Philippa's rooms, located in the imposing east turret of the castle.

I chewed on the fudge brownie cupcake she'd stuffed in my mouth and avoided paying any attention to what sounded like disembodied whispers in the shadows. After all, there was no such thing as ghosts.

"Granny, it's only us," Alice called out. "I've brought Holly and cake with me."

"How exciting!" Lady Philippa said from inside her main living room.

Alice pushed open the door, and I followed with the tea tray balanced in my hands.

My eyebrows shot up as I took in the tight lurid orange, green, and pink Lycra outfit Lady Philippa wore.

"I always thought pink was your color." Alice pressed a kiss to her granny's cheek.

Lady Philippa tugged at the seam of the leotard. "I thought this would be more comfortable. The back of this thing keeps riding up. I'll be chafed by the end of the day. And I thought it was supposed to be sweat absorbing. I'm not sure Lycra is for me."

"Holly wears a lot of Lycra." Alice dropped into the squashy red velvet armchair by the window. "She's always trying out some sort of exercise. I get tired just looking at her."

"Have you got any tips to make this thing more comfortable?" Lady Philippa tugged at the gusset of her leotard. "I've even shaken some talc inside the pants, but they still rub my thighs."

I bit my lip and concentrated on setting out the tea and cakes. "I prefer comfy tracksuit bottoms and oversized T-shirts to Lycra. I've never been a fan. It's not very forgiving on the figure."

"I should say," Lady Philippa said. "It shows all the lumps and bumps. I'll be back in a second. I need to change into something much more forgiving if I'm to eat all that cake." She hurried into her bedroom and returned a few moments later in a floor length green silk kimono. "That's so much better. Everything is free. My wobbly bits are allowed to move as nature intended." She grabbed a large fudge brownie cupcake as she settled in her own seat.

"Come sit." Alice patted the chair next to her. "Don't stand on ceremony. It's just us."

I joined them and poured out the tea.

"Everyone's started arriving for the anniversary party tomorrow," Alice said. "The place is going to be so noisy. And Caroline never stops talking."

"I'm looking forward to seeing them all." Lady Philippa leaned closer to me. "And for once, I'm being allowed out of my prison. We have to put on a good appearance for the rest of the family."

"You know the rules. You can come out if you're on your best behavior," Alice said, not the hint of a joke in her voice. "No scaring people with your wild theories and pointing out all the ghosts in the castle."

"The ghosts will be no bother at the party," Lady Philippa said. "They dislike chatter and noise. I expect most of them will stay up here. They like it in the turret because I talk to them."

"That's a good thing," Alice said. "Henrietta doesn't need any excuse to avoid the party. I know she's dreading it. I heard her crying in her room when I passed the door. I knocked to see if I could do anything to help, but she pretended she wasn't in there."

"Poor sweet Henrietta." Lady Philippa shook her head. "The oldest girl and still not married. In my day, the others wouldn't have been permitted to marry until she'd found herself a suitable husband."

Alice burst out in laughter. "That's not true."

"It absolutely is. The oldest first, before the others are presented and can find themselves a man."

Alice chortled as she ate some cake. "Henrietta's single because she prefers her book boyfriends to real men. Although the way Jane Austen writes about that Mr. Darcy, I can understand. I've never met anyone like him."

"I always thought he was a bit grumpy," Lady Philippa said. "I need a man who can make me laugh so much my stomach aches. Henrietta would benefit from getting her nose out of a book and looking at the world around her. There's a lot of fun to be had."

Alice sighed. "Much like me, I expect she's resigned to life as a spinster."

"You're not a spinster," Lady Philippa said. "You're not even thirty. I'll have you married off yet. Forget your past engagements. Those men weren't right for you."

Alice's blue eyes twinkled. "Do you see that in my future, Granny? Is my husband-to-be very handsome? Does he own a big yacht?"

"Looks and big boats aren't important. Finding a man who adores you, makes you smile, and tells you how stunning and incredible you are every day is what you want."

Even I had to sigh at that, and I wasn't a hopeless romantic.

"So, when do you see me marrying?" Alice asked.

"Not yet. But I'll tell you when the time is right." Lady Philippa patted the notepad beside her. "I hear that Mary couldn't make it."

Alice touched my knee. "Mary's an adventurer. She travels the world taking photographs. She's very good at it. She even has several galleries who showcase her work and is often the main attraction at different photography events. My cousin is talented. I wish I could take a good snap. My pictures always come out fuzzy."

"That's because you're always bouncing around," Lady Philippa said. "But you're right about Mary. She knows how to seek out adventure."

"She's fearless about everything," Alice said. "Including not caring what other people think of her. It can make her a bit … I'm not sure how to describe her."

"Opinionated and not afraid to tell you what's on her mind," Lady Philippa said. "She keeps me thoroughly entertained when she's around. If she hasn't upset everyone in the room by the end of a social event, she thinks she's failed. But I'm rather glad she's not here to spoil Diana and Percy's anniversary dinner."

"We don't want any drama," Alice said. "Just lots of fun. And of course, plenty of delicious food. What have you made for the party, Holly?"

"Nothing. I'm sticking to making the café food," I said. "It's best if I keep out of the way of the party food."

"You don't want to cater for the event?" Lady Philippa asked.

"Holly's made an enemy." Alice waggled her eyebrows. "Can you believe it?"

"An enemy? Who wouldn't like our Holly?"

"The baker making the anniversary cake," Alice said. "Lorcan Blaze. It was so funny, they did a taste test and he was so sure he'd win. Holly beat him hands down with her desserts. Lorcan was fuming. His face was bright red. I thought steam would fly out of his ears."

Lady Philippa chuckled as she ate more cake. "I've no doubt your food would beat his. My advice, stay out of his way. He sounds like a bad lot. You don't need somebody in your life who makes things difficult."

"I couldn't agree more," I said. "And talking of difficult people, do either of you know Percy's friend, Blaine? He drives a flashy red sports car."

"I should say," Alice said. "If there's one word to describe Blaine Masters, it's yuck. He's a show off, a bore, and a womanizer. The last time we met at a social event, he tried to get me in the broom closet so he could have his wicked way with me."

Lady Philippa almost snorted tea out of her nose. "Did you let him? Is he terribly good-looking?"

"Oh, he's handsome enough. He's got that classic dark chiseled look. He's also very tall, and I love a tall man. But his looks are wiped away by his terrible personality. He's always claiming to have done something amazing or been to the latest event. He loves to be seen in the right places."

Lady Philippa grabbed the notebook from the table next to her. "Did you say Blaine Masters?"

"That's right," Alice said.

Lady Philippa ran her finger down the page in her notebook. "We won't have to worry about him for much longer. He'll be dead soon."

My mouth dropped open.

Alice giggled. "Pay no attention, Holly. It's just another of Granny's funny predictions."

"Someone dying isn't funny," I said.

Alice pursed her lips. "He's really going to die?"

"Oh yes, it's in my book," Lady Philippa said. "I'd forgotten about it until you said his name and it jogged my memory."

"What's going to happen to him?" I asked.

"I didn't get the details of his demise," Lady Philippa said. "It sounds as if it won't be a loss if he's no longer with us."

"Granny! That's a dreadful thing to say," Alice said. "Although he is terribly smarmy. The way he looks at you, it's like he's undressing you with his eyes. No matter how many layers I have on, I always feel like he knows exactly what's underneath my clothes. It's most unsettling."

"If you're certain he's going to die, we need to warn him," I said. "Stop it from happening."

"How can we do that if we don't know what's going to happen to him?" Alice said. "He could be run over, choke on an olive, have a brick land on his head, be bitten by a poisonous snake. We'd have to wrap him in a duvet and hide him in a room to make sure he didn't die."

"Then he might suffocate inside the duvet," Lady Philippa said.

"We should still tell him," I said. "Make sure he knows to be careful when he's driving or doesn't drink too much. Anything we can to keep him safe."

"Hmmm, I don't know about that. It would be an awkward conversation," Alice said. "Blaine, you're going to die. We have no idea how, when, where, or why, but get your affairs in order. Good luck."

"It wouldn't have to be like that. You know him," I said. "You could say something. Maybe you could say you had a feeling about him and needed to make sure he was safe."

Alice grimaced. "I wouldn't dream of saying anything like that to Blaine. He'd misinterpret it and think I wanted to go to his bedroom and have silly fun with him. That's never going to happen. Blaine Masters must fend for himself."

A high-pitched, frantic yipping came from the bedroom. Horatio bowled out, glancing over his shoulder as he sped toward Lady Philippa.

"What's the matter?" She reached down and scooped the overweight corgi onto her lap, where he sat trembling. "Are the ghosts acting up again?"

Alice exchanged an amused glance with me. "They're always teasing Horatio. It's a good thing too. That lazy old dog wouldn't get out of bed if it weren't for the ghosts prodding him with their icy fingers."

I glanced at the bedroom door. I wanted to run over and shut it in the hope it would keep whatever was in there away from us.

"I understand that you're not a fan of Blaine's," I said, "but maybe you could keep an eye on him at the party, just to make sure he doesn't get himself in trouble. If we can prevent a death happening here, that's a good thing."

"Even if it's Blaine Masters?" Alice arched an eyebrow.

"He might not be a nice guy, but I don't want him dead." I hesitated. He had almost run me over. Maybe this was karma coming back to give him a final kick in the behind. "Keep watch over him tomorrow night. You don't have to say anything. It might be all we need to make sure he's safe."

Lady Philippa fed a piece of cake to Horatio, which he munched down in two noisy bites. "My predictions are never wrong. Nothing you can do will change the situation."

"They're often wrong," Alice said. "You predicted it would be a sunny day on my birthday. It rained the whole time."

"My important predictions are always accurate," Lady Philippa said.

"The weather on my birthday was crucially important," Alice said. "I planned a whole day outside. A picnic, boating on the lake, croquet on the lawn. It was all ruined. Holly, pay no attention to Granny's predictions. I'm certain she makes most of this up."

Lady Philippa raised an eyebrow as she stared at me. "Holly can make her own mind up. We have an understanding."

I jumped as the bedroom door slammed shut. "I'd better go." I stood, my nerves jangling. The ghosts, which I did not believe in, had seen me off.

"You're welcome to stay," Lady Philippa said. "But we're only going to be talking about boring family things. Mainly the party and if I can get away with my daisy yellow tracksuit."

"Just you dare wear that. Diana will be mortified," Alice said.

"It could be quite fun. I'd be the center of attention."

Alice dissolved into giggles. "We should both wear tracksuits. Diana would hate that, and I could eat as much cake as I like and not worry about squeezing into my dress."

"Thanks for the tea and cake," I said. I went to pet Horatio's head, but he growled at me.

"Take no notice of him," Lady Philippa said. "He always gets in a bad mood when he's been spooked by the ghosts."

I nodded goodbye to Alice before hurrying out of the turret and down the long twisty flight of stone steps.

Despite Alice telling me I should ignore Lady Philippa's warning about Blaine's death, I felt that I had to do something. If he was in danger, perhaps I could help. Was there a way I could warn Blaine without looking insane and risk losing my job if word got around that I was whispering about death in peoples' ears?

I entered the main hall of the castle and slowed. Campbell and Saracen were on duty, standing outside an entrance to the private family rooms.

There were no visitors around, so I risked going over, even though they were on duty and I shouldn't disturb them.

"Hi, Saracen. I've been baking a new kind of cookie for you to try."

His gaze slid to Campbell, who hadn't moved. "That sounds good. Although the last ones you gave me were great."

Ever since I'd learned about Saracen's diabetes, I'd been testing alternatives to the cookies and cakes he used to overindulge in. It had been hit and miss, but I was finding success with cookies sweetened with fruit and using very dark chocolate with low levels of sugar.

"These are sweetened with dates, and I've been trying different kinds of nuts. Walnuts seem to work the best. I'll have to bring you a batch."

Campbell grunted and flicked his fingers toward me.

I tilted my head and glared at him. "Am I supposed to understand what that gesture means?"

"It means we're working," he muttered.

"It means he's jealous because you're not making him special cookies." Saracen grinned.

"No distractions. We're on the job."

"There's no one around," I said. "It's safe to exchange a few pleasantries."

Campbell made the same gesture with his hand.

Saracen pulled back his shoulders and nodded at me. "I look forward to trying your cookies, Holly."

"You're very welcome," I said. "But none for you, Campbell. I'm only being friendly."

He responded by clasping his hands behind his back.

Gah! Today wasn't my day for interacting with people. I was glad I had the rest of the afternoon off work so I couldn't lock horns with anyone else.

I turned and strode away. For the rest of the day, I'd curl up on my couch, binge watch box sets, and snuggle with Meatball, while eating too much pecan pie and ice cream. That was all the company and entertainment I needed to make me happy.

I jerked upright in my bed and yanked off my sleep mask.

Meatball whined and jumped onto the bed before licking my hand.

My senses were on high alert, but I couldn't figure out what had woken me. I looked around the gloom of my bedroom. Everything felt still and peaceful.

I jumped as a thudding sounded on my front door and checked the time. It was four o'clock in the morning! Who was trying to get inside my apartment at this time?

I shuffled out of bed, stuffed my feet into my slippers, and grabbed my robe before hurrying to the front door. Before I opened it, I peered out the window by the side of the door. Chef Heston stood outside, his fist raised, ready to hit the door again.

I pulled it open. "Is everything okay?"

"Good, you're awake. I've been knocking for ages. We have a situation." He ran a hand down his face, his hair sticking out in un-brushed peaks.

"Is there something wrong with the kitchen? Has there been a fire?"

"Nothing like that. The kitchen is fine." He scrubbed at his forehead with his fingers.

"Then what is it?" I tightened my robe around my waist. The tension radiating off Chef Heston made me twitchy.

"It's Lorcan. He's got food poisoning."

"Oh! I'm sorry to hear that." Actually, a small part of me wasn't at all sorry. I couldn't wish food poisoning on a more ideal candidate.

"So am I. With Lorcan sick, he won't be able to finish the cake for the anniversary party."

"I imagine not. Food poisoning takes it out of you."

"Which is why you're going to help."

I took a step back. "You want me to make the anniversary cake?"

"You're the best I've got, Holly. I need you. Get dressed. We have to get baking right away."

Chapter 4

I downed my fourth mug of coffee and stifled a yawn. I was operating on caffeine and low-level fear. I'd been frantically baking, whipping icing, and practicing cake decorations for the last four hours, alongside Chef Heston.

The early morning kitchen staff had arrived at six o'clock, and everyone had been surprised to see us there.

Chef Heston had warned them off with growls and sharp comments if anyone dared ask what we were doing.

Despite being mildly terrified about working so closely with Chef Heston, it had gone well. He concentrated on making the first five layers of the seven-layer sky rise cake for the party, and I focused on the presentation and the final two layers.

Sally and Louise, two talented members of the kitchen team, snuck over the second Chef Heston disappeared to grab more ingredients from the kitchen store.

"You look busy," Sally said. "What are you working on?"

I took a step back and studied the dozens of yellow and white flower decorations I'd been slaving over. "These go on the base the anniversary cake sits on."

"They look stunning." Louise nodded and smiled. "You're doing the party cake now? That's impressive."

I blew out a breath. "Yup. Seven layers of cake. The first two layers have an intricate design of gold and black lines, then the next three layers are dotted in gold, and the top two layers will be showered in gold glitter."

Sally wrinkled her nose. "Too much gold and not enough filling for my liking. What are the cakes made of?"

"They're having seven different types of cake. Each layer will be unique."

"Typical," Louise said. "Why can't they settle for a delicious sponge and be done with it?"

I grinned. "Where's the challenge in that?"

"Go on, make us drool. What's in each layer?" Sally asked.

"At the base we have fruit cake, then Battenberg, lemon, classic Victoria sponge, chocolate, cherry, and finally vanilla and raspberry."

"I've just put on half a stone hearing about all that cake." Sally looked around the kitchen. "I thought Lorcan was making the cake for the party. Where is he?"

"He got food poisoning last night," I said. "We've had to start from scratch, just in case it was the cake that made him sick."

"He was taste testing a lot of raw ingredients when he was in here yesterday," Sally said. "I saw him lick the spoon twice. Maybe the eggs were dodgy."

Louise grinned. "It serves him right. I couldn't believe it when he challenged you over your food and then acted as if he'd made a mistake. I knew then he was a wrong one."

I set down my icing bag and rolled my shoulders, glad to have a few minutes break. "His food was nice. I'd have paid money for it."

"But it wasn't a patch on yours," Louise said. "We all know that. And now you get to make the party cake. This will give you huge exposure. And have you seen the parking lot? It's full of Bentleys, limousines, and Jaguars. The great and fabulously wealthy will be at the party tonight. When they learn you made this amazing cake, you might get some freelance work. Imagine that. You could be baking for other influential families, or sent around the world first class to whip up brownies and cupcakes for royalty. What a dream."

I tilted my head as I pondered the idea. I didn't hate that thought, but I loved what I did at the castle. "I need to get this one right before anything like that happens. If I get the layers uneven on this cake and it collapses, no one will want me to make them toast, let alone anything fancy."

Sally patted my arm. "Good luck. Not that you need it. I've got to get on. I've got two hundred sausage rolls that need to be made and baked."

"Me too, although I'm on peeling duty." Louise made a face before they both hurried away.

Chef Heston strode over, a frown on his face and his phone in his hand. "If Lorcan sends me one more rude text about how things are going, I may just blow a gasket."

I looked at the text message on his phone. *Send me pictures. How long did you whisk the sponge for? Remember it has to be large eggs for the fruit base.*

Chef Heston deleted the message. "He's behaving as if I have no idea how to make a basic cake."

"This is his cake baby," I said. "He wants it to go well."

"He lost the privilege of sticking his nose in when he got sick." Chef Heston shook his head. "Still, I won't have to worry about his demanding messages anymore. I've given him your number and told him you're in charge."

I sagged against the counter. "But I'm not! I don't want him bothering me while I make the rest of the decorations."

"Likewise. And it's over to you now, anyway. I've done the five bases. You just need to finish the last two and add the decorations."

"All the flowers, the hand piping, and the glitter?" My hand went to my stomach.

He slapped me on the shoulder. "Exactly. No more than a few hours of work."

"A few hours! This would normally take days to complete."

"I know you, Holly. You can never resist a challenge."

"What about the rest of my duties in the kitchen?"

"I've divided them among everyone else. They'll get done. Your one and only task is to get this cake right." He pulled his phone out again. "Here's some close-up pictures of the finished product. I'm sending them to you."

I checked my phone as the messages pinged in with the attachments. I opened one and studied the beautiful gold and white cake. It would be a challenge, but I could do it.

"How's Lorcan doing? If he's sending these messages, he must be feeling better," I said.

"He's sick as a dog." Chef Heston grimaced. "I sent someone up to see how he was feeling and if he wanted anything to eat. He yelled at them and threw a shoe at their head. I'm not risking sending any more of my staff to see him until he learns to behave himself." He strode away, grumbling to himself.

I turned and looked at the half-finished cake. Excitement bubbled inside me as well as a fair amount of nerves. If I got this right, it would be a great accolade. But if I got it wrong … I shook my head. No, I wouldn't think like that. Most of the cake was made, just the easy small sponges to bake, and the decorations to finish.

The kitchen door was pulled open. A tall man with dark wavy hair and a warm smile walked in with a pretty blonde who I immediately recognized as an Audley from her coloring.

They both looked around the kitchen as if trying to find somebody.

I wiped my hands on a cloth before walking over. "May I help you?"

"I do hope so," the woman said. "I wanted to see how my cake was coming on. Is it ready yet?"

"Oh! You must be Lady Diana?"

She flashed me a smile. "That's right. And this is my husband, Percy Phipps. I'm so excited to see my wedding cake brought back to life. It was such a happy day, wasn't it darling?"

Percy nodded. "It was a very happy day."

"And we want to recreate it all again, including my cake. I was looking for Lorcan. I'd hoped he'd almost finished so I could get an advance preview," Lady Diana said.

I glanced over my shoulder but couldn't see Chef Heston. "I'm sorry to give you bad news, but Lorcan was taken ill last night."

Lady Diana's eyes filled with tears, and she turned her husband. "We must have a cake. Percy, do something."

"Oh, don't worry, we have a backup plan," I said. "I've been working with the castle chef. He's excellent at what he does. We've made a new cake for you."

"A new cake?" Lady Diana sniffed and her gaze ran over me. "You and some unknown chef are making my precious anniversary cake? I don't know if I approve. This is the first I've heard of these unplanned changes."

"I'm sure it'll be wonderful." Percy tucked an arm around his wife's shoulders. "Whatever you can make at such short notice will be appreciated."

Lady Diana shook her head. "I wanted our cake. Lorcan Blaze made our wedding cake, and I wanted him to make our anniversary cake. It's important to me that everything is perfect."

"I'll make it as perfect as possible," I said. "Come and see what we've made so far. You can even taste some. We've worked to the exact recipe that Lorcan provided and have dozens of pictures from your actual wedding cake to ensure it looks as similar as possible."

"I don't want similar, I want the same," Lady Diana said.

Any second now, she was going to stamp her foot and pout.

"Let's take a look," Percy said. "We might be surprised."

"I hope you are. Please, come this way. It's not finished yet, and we've got two more layers to complete, but most of the decorations are done. Once the final layers are baked, they need to cool, then I can put everything together."

"It sounds like you've worked hard," Percy said. "Thank you for making such an effort for us. I'm sorry, I don't know your name."

"It was my pleasure," I said. "I'm Holly Holmes."

"Who have you baked for?" Lady Diana asked.

"I used to run a café in Audley St. Mary, so most of the villagers have sampled my food. I specialize in desserts."

"A café! You haven't made cakes for anyone famous?"

"I provide cakes to the Audley family on a daily basis if that counts."

Lady Diana's nose lifted in the air. "I suppose it counts for something. Very well, let's take a look at what you've done."

Nerves rattled through me as I led them to the table where my decorations were laid out, and the five layers of cake stood waiting to be stacked, iced, and decorated.

"May I?" Percy gestured to the flower decorations on the table.

"Yes! Take a closer look. I always make spares just in case any break while the cake is being put together," I said.

Percy lifted a yellow flower decoration and studied it. "Your attention to detail is remarkable. And you've done this on your own?"

"Most of the decorations. I enjoy doing it," I said.

"Look at this, darling." He held the flower out for Lady Diana.

"I suppose it does look similar to what was on our wedding cake. Do you think our guests will notice the difference?"

"They'll be too busy drinking champagne and dancing to worry about the cake. You were the one who wanted the wedding cake again. I'd have been happy with anything delicious."

Lady Diana sighed. "You act as if you don't care about our anniversary party."

"You know that's not true. I want you to be happy."

"If you have any suggestions or changes you'd like before I put the cake together, please let me know." I pulled my phone out and opened a picture of the cake. "This is what I'm working toward. It'll look just like this."

Lady Diana stared at the picture. "I just don't want anyone to say anything bad about our party. What if people learn that Lorcan didn't make our cake?"

"All that matters is that we enjoy ourselves," Percy said. "That's what this is about, not pleasing our friends and family."

"Blaine will only stir things up if he knows something's gone wrong."

"Blaine Masters?" The name shot out of my mouth before I could stop myself.

"That's right. Do you know Blaine?" Lady Diana looked skeptical.

"Well, I wouldn't say I know him. We've met."

She chuckled. "Every woman knows Blaine. He's the world's most outrageous flirt."

"Oh, no! I don't know him like that," I said. "We met on the road to the castle. His ... erratic driving caught my attention."

Percy shook his head. "That's typical Blaine. He always has to be seen driving the most powerful car."

"I bet he had some woman with him," Lady Diana said.

"He did," I said. "I saw her long dark hair as they passed me."

"I only gave him a plus one because he likes to have a pretty little thing on his arm at social events." Lady Diana shook her head. "Blaine needs to grow up and settle down. Percy was a wild child when we first met, but I soon tamed him."

Percy pursed his lips, and he cleared his throat. "I wouldn't say that, my dear."

"You were always out drinking and gallivanting. It wasn't until you met me that you realized how wonderful it was to have a partner."

He glanced at me and adjusted his collar. "Your work on our cake is excellent. Thank you so much. I'm sure it'll be delicious. I look forward to having several pieces tonight."

"One piece," Lady Diana said. "I need to watch your waistline. You've already gone up a pants size since we got married."

"Let's go for a walk, shall we? It sounds like I need to burn off some calories." Percy said goodbye before leading Lady Diana out of the kitchen.

My initial excitement about making the cake had faded during that conversation. Lady Diana wasn't at all impressed that I was making her cake.

Fair enough. I was no big shot chef with a worldwide reputation for excellent cakes, but I knew my way around a recipe.

I turned back to the counter and looked at my list of tasks. I had everything in order. All I needed to do was follow the steps, and I would create perfection. I'd blow Lady Diana away with how amazing my cake was. It would be even better than Lorcan Blaze's original masterpiece.

I sat on the bench beside the castle wall near the kitchen door and closed my eyes, tipping my head back and enjoying the feeling of the warm late afternoon sun on my skin.

Meatball sat next to me, chewing on a milk bone as I took a five-minute break from the frantic activity in the kitchen.

My eyes stung, my neck felt tight, and my arm muscles were sore from all the beating of cake batter and icing. But the sky rise cake was coming together. I'd been working on it for twelve hours.

Chef Heston had dipped in and out to help, but his attention was taken with running the rest of the kitchen. But I could see a light at the end of this sweet, challenging tunnel of sponge, fruit cake, and Battenberg.

"Excuse me. I think I'm lost."

I opened my eyes to discover a chunky ginger man standing in front of me. He wore beige tweed and a pink shirt that highlighted the ruddiness of his cheeks.

"What are you looking for?" I asked. "This area isn't of any interest to visitors to the castle."

"I'm not a tourist," he said. "I'm with the anniversary party. I'm James Postle. I've been walking around for half an hour trying to find the organic fruit garden. Diana told me where it was, but I'm not sure her directions were spot on. I headed out of the castle, turned left and then left again, then everything went wrong. I ended up by some compost heaps and storage sheds. In the end, I traced my steps back until I found the castle and figured if I hugged the wall I'd find the right place. This definitely isn't an organic fruit garden."

Meatball poked his head over the table as he assessed the visitor.

"You're about half a mile in the wrong direction," I said.

"Ah, I see." James peered down at Meatball. "Is that dog yours?"

"He is. He's friendly if you want to pet him."

Meatball wagged his tail, and his ears pricked up. "Woof woof."

"What a handsome chap." James strode around the bench and engaged in some extreme rubbing with Meatball, much to his delirious delight.

I grinned as I watched them tussle. "I take it you like dogs?"

"I love them. I've got six setters back home. I couldn't bring them with me; they're absolutely bonkers, full of energy and always on the go. I take them out walking for three hours every day. I adore them. Such clever animals. This one looks like he's got the smarts about him too."

"Meatball is a one-of-a-kind," I said.

"Meatball! What a fun name. He's like a little round barrel of joy."

Meatball flopped onto his side and exposed his belly for more rubbing, which James obliged him with.

"How do you know the happy couple?" I asked.

"I was Percy's best man at their wedding," James said. "We grew up together. We went to the same school and have always been tight. I was thrilled when he asked me to be best man. I can't believe they've been together for five years."

"It's been a happy five years?" I asked.

He scratched a hand through his short ginger hair. "It's hard to judge how good a relationship is when you're looking at it from the outside. Percy seems happy most of the time. I get the impression that if he does everything Diana tells him, life is good. What's the saying, happy wife, happy life? I think that's the motto he lives by."

"They were in the kitchen earlier today. I'm helping to make their anniversary cake."

"Oh! You bake? How exciting. I can't cook a thing. I've never had to, always had people who do that sort of thing for me, but I'm envious of people who can create delicious things in the kitchen. Do you have a speciality?"

"Well, anything sweet. I make an excellent cupcake."

"I love cupcakes. I love all cakes as you may have noticed." He patted his round stomach. "I shouldn't overindulge. In fact, I need to get myself in shape and start looking for a wife of my own. I'm the same age as Percy, so it's time I settle down. The problem is, the ladies don't often go for ginger hair and pot bellies. I can't understand it myself." He laughed good-naturedly.

"Personality is the most important thing," I said. "Looks fade. If you have a kind nature and a good way about you that will appeal to lots of women."

He gave a nod. "If only that were true in my social circles. The ladies like a firm jaw, a six pack, and a healthy bank balance. Sadly, I've only got one of those things. I need to cast my net further afield. I don't suppose you know of any friendly single gals who don't mind a bit of ginger in their life?"

"Not many," I said. My thoughts turned briefly to Alice. What would she think of James?

"I don't suppose you're single, are you? A pretty thing like you who knows her way around the kitchen would be a catch."

A blush rose to my cheeks. "Actually, I am single. I love my work a bit too much to keep a relationship going. Love me, love my baking."

He blinked several times. "Why on earth haven't you been scooped off the shelf and married to some handsome chap a long time ago?"

A laugh shot out, and my face grew hot. "You must be looking forward to the anniversary party."

"It's always good to celebrate a friend's happiness," he said.

"Do you know Blaine Masters?"

His forehead wrinkled before he nodded. "I do. Blaine's done some business with Percy in the past. They met at university. How do you know him?"

"Oh, I bumped into him here." Or rather, he literally bumped into me.

"Ah! He always has an eye for the pretty women." James chuckled and looked away.

"He did seem a little ... full of himself. I wouldn't describe him as chivalrous."

James' eyes tightened. "I hope he did nothing to offend you."

"In a way, he did." I gently touched my scraped knee. "What do you think of him?"

James stood from petting Meatball and rocked back on his heels. "Your description was accurate. Blaine is full of himself. He likes to talk big but is rarely a man who follows through with any action. Honestly, I'm not a big fan. I steer clear when we're at gatherings like this party. You know, he even tried to have me fired."

"He wanted you to lose your job?"

James chortled. "No, from my role as best man to Percy."

"What did he do?"

James looked around before blowing out a breath. "We'd all gone out, a big group of us, to celebrate Percy asking Diana to marry him. Everyone was in high spirits, and the drink was flowing. I'd only had a couple of drinks, when I began to feel strange. The next thing, I'm waking up five hours later back at the hotel. I passed out. It was humiliating."

"Did Blaine have something to do with that?"

"I can only think it was him. Although I have no proof. He got in a round of drinks and was deliberate about making sure I got a specific glass. He put something in that drink that knocked me out."

"He drugged you! That's illegal."

"There wasn't anything I could do about it. Then I heard that Blaine was suggesting to Percy that I wasn't fit for the job of best man because I couldn't handle my alcohol."

"What did Percy think about that?"

"Fortunately for me, Percy dismissed the whole idea. I was glad he did. I was proud to be his best man, and I didn't appreciate Blaine trying to spoil things. He's always so eager to curry favor with Percy. I think he's after his connections rather than his friendship, which is simply wrong. You make a friend because you like a person, not because they can open doors for you."

Everything I heard about Blaine made me dislike him a bit more.

"Holly! There you are." Rupert strolled out through the kitchen door, his hands shoved in his pants pockets.

"Rupert Audley! How the devil are you?" James strode over, and there was much backslapping and handshaking.

"Very well, thanks. I see you've met our amazing baker, Holly."

"I was just getting to know her." James turned to me and smiled. "She seems like a charming lady."

The smile on Rupert's face faded. "She is that. I recently took Holly to a goat sanctuary for the day. We had a nice time together."

"A goat sanctuary! I've never heard of such a thing. Is that your idea of a romantic date?" James roared a laugh. "You might need to up your dating ideas, old man."

Rupert scratched the back of his head. "It wasn't so much a date. Or was it, Holly?"

This was shifting into awkward territory too fast for my liking. I hopped from my seat and scooped up Meatball. "I'll leave you to catch up. I've got an anniversary cake to finish. I hope you both enjoy the party this evening." I dashed away before I got into any more conversation about my was-it-or-wasn't-it a date at the goat sanctuary with Rupert.

I settled Meatball in his kennel before heading back into the kitchen, washing up, and then turning to the cake.

This was it. I needed one last push to get the sky rise cake together. All the decorations had been made, the layers were iced in pristine snow white icing, and now it needed to be constructed.

Chef Heston marched over. "Ready to go?"

I nodded. "Let's do this."

The next hour was one of the most intense situations I'd ever experienced. I had not only Chef Heston breathing down my neck and watching my every move as I put the cake together, but several of the kitchen staff stopped working to watch.

"Steady with that final layer," Chef Heston said. "It has to be exactly even or the whole thing will collapse."

My tongue poked between my teeth as I eased the final layer of sky rise cake into place. I pressed it down gently, using a fondant glue to make sure it stuck. I held it for a full minute, barely breathing.

I stepped back and studied the cake, looking for any defect with the levels.

Chef Heston patted my shoulder. "Good job, Holly. All you have to do now is decorate it."

Any normal person would want to collapse on the floor at this point, but for me, this was the fun part. I always loved to decorate.

I whirled around the cake, placing the handcrafted flowers around the base, piping on the colors, and ending with an impressive shower of edible gold glitter over the top that cascaded down the side like a magical waterfall.

Several people clapped as I placed down the glitter sieve. I turned and grinned as I saw my friends looking on with appreciation.

"Great job," Sally said. "I'd be scared to eat that. It looks too good to destroy with a knife."

"The guests had better eat the whole thing," I said. "All this work for them not to touch it, I'd be devastated."

"They won't be able to resist," Louise said. "And you'd better get a bonus in your pay packet for this extra work. I heard that Chef dragged you out of bed before dawn so this would be done in time."

I glanced over at Chef Heston. He sometimes surprised me with little bonuses when I did a good job.

He lifted his head and met my gaze. "All done?"

I nodded. "Come take a look. See if I've missed anything."

He strode over and spent an agonizing five minutes walking around the cake. At one point, he even pulled out a tape measure and measured from the base to the top and then each layer one by one. With a satisfied grunt, he put his tape measure away.

"If that doesn't make Lady Diana happy, I don't know what will. Make sure you're ready when it's time to present the cake to the party."

My stomach flipped. "You want me involved in that?" Chef Heston often attended the parties to showcase the incredible food we served. I'd never been invited to join him.

"Of course. Your hard work means our joint success. You deserve to be acknowledged for this." He walked away, humming under his breath.

Louise and Sally both grinned at me.

"Get you," Sally said. "Being presented to the family and all their posh friends. I hope you've got a nice dress to wear."

I looked down at my flour splattered clothing. "No! I didn't even think about getting changed."

"At least wipe the gold glitter off your face." Louise dabbed a thumb on my cheek.

"Right! Yes, good plan." With the cake done, there was nothing left for me to do. A big part of me wanted to flop into bed and not move for a week, but I was excited to see what the guests at the party thought of the cake.

I dashed back to my apartment and took half an hour to make myself presentable. I'd had no time for a shower this morning, so hopped in and out in five minutes, dried my hair until it was smooth and sleek around my head, and applied a little makeup, before putting on a clean uniform.

I looked at myself in the mirror and nodded. There was tiredness beneath my eyes, but it had been worth it. I wanted to burst with pride over how incredible the cake had turned out.

I walked back into the kitchen just as the cake was being placed on its base on a large silver trolley. My breath caught in my throat as the cake rocked.

"Be careful!" Chef Heston roared as he supervised the move. "I will string you up by your ears outside the castle walls if you ruin this."

"Sorry, Chef," the kitchen assistant, Johnny, said.

Chef Heston noticed me and nodded. "Time to move."

I walked beside him, my stomach a riot of nerves as he pushed the cake toward the north quarter and the dining parlor. The parlor, the great drawing room, and the little drawing room had been opened exclusively for the anniversary party.

Two security guards stood outside the door of the great drawing room in tuxedos. It was Kace Delaney and Mason Sloane on duty tonight, both looking impressive in their outfits.

"Open up. We've got the cake for the party," Chef Heston said.

Mason nodded, and they both pushed open the double doors.

A riot of noise, laughter, and music hit me.

"Are you coming in?" Chef Heston glanced over his shoulder.

I hadn't realized I'd stopped walking. I sucked in a deep breath and followed him in, clasping my hands behind my back.

We waited by the door until an attendant in a white tuxedo and matching gloves approached us.

"One moment, please. The music will fade, and then you are to present the cake in the center of the room. Lady Diana will attend to you."

My stomach tightened. Everyone would see us. "Are you sure it's okay that I'm here?" I whispered to Chef Heston.

"Of course. But no talking. Just watch, and you'll be fine," he said. "Enjoy this moment, Holly. You earned it."

"You're here!" Alice bounded over and flung an arm around my shoulders before kissing my cheek. She wore a stunning off the shoulder amber dress that fell to the floor, revealing her incredible curves. "Oh, Holly! The cake looks out of this world amazing."

"Thanks. I hope Lady Diana and Percy like it," I said.

"If they don't, they're idiots. Actually, Diana can be an idiot at times, so just ignore her if she complains about something."

The music died, and the attendant gestured us forward.

I walked into the center of the room where the crowd had parted to make way for us. Chef Heston stopped and stood back from the cake, gesturing for me to do the same.

The crowd oohed and aahed as Lady Diana and Percy approached.

Percy looked gorgeous in a tailored black tuxedo. His dark hair was swept off his face, and that same easy smile I'd seen him with before made him look warm and approachable.

Lady Diana looked equally incredible. She had a glittering tiara immersed in the curls on her head and dramatic dark eye makeup to match her midnight blue gown.

There was silence for a full thirty seconds, and I counted each one as they looked at the cake.

Lady Diana clapped her hands together and smiled. "Isn't it stunning? Our wedding cake brought back to life to celebrate five glorious years of marriage."

I blew out a breath at the same time as Chef Heston. We shared a brief smile.

"Excellent work," Percy said. "It's like I'm back at my wedding day all over again."

The crowd applauded politely.

Lady Diana held her hand out, not looking at Chef Heston.

He produced a knife from beneath the trolley and handed it to her.

"Make sure you get plenty of pictures of us together, everybody." She gestured at Percy.

He slid into place behind her, circled her waist with his arms, and they cut into the bottom layer of the cake.

There was more applause and cheering.

"Take it to the serving table and prepare it for our guests." Lady Diana handed the knife back to Chef Heston. "Make sure to leave the top tier for us."

He inclined his head before wheeling the cake to a table laden with delicate canapes and filled vol au vents.

I rolled my shoulders as I followed him. Who'd have thought that presenting cakes would be so stressful? I was more back room than front of house, and that suited me just fine.

Chef Heston passed me the knife. "Since you helped to make it, why don't you start cutting it up?"

"Thanks. I'd love to." I set to work on dismantling the layers of cake before slicing off chunks of fruit cake, lemon sponge, and chocolate cake. Guests were soon strolling over to grab a slice.

The Duchess walked over, a glass of champagne in her hand. She looked incredible in an oyster pink gown that rippled when she moved. "I'm in awe of your cake making skills, Holly. I had Diana in tears in my room for almost an hour earlier today because she was worried the cake wouldn't be good enough. I told her all about your brilliant baking skills. And as I can see for myself, you've done us proud."

"It was a joint effort," I said. "Chef Heston made most of the cakes. I focused on the decorating."

"Of course. Our brilliant chef." She smiled brightly at Chef Heston who stood a few steps away. "Thank you, both of you. I always try to keep my daughters happy, but

Diana's always been so precise about things. She always has to have everything just so. I sometimes think I overindulged her when she was young. But you always want to overindulge your children, don't you?"

I was just the same with Meatball, so I understood. "Would you like a piece of cake?"

"I'll take two slices of the lemon, please. I've lost sight of my husband. No doubt he's studying an oil painting somewhere in the castle and trying to remember which relative it is. I might be able to entice him back to the party with the promise of cake."

I handed her two large slices before cutting up more cake for the eager party guests.

"Blaine! We must have cake." A shrill female voice caught my attention, as did the name she said.

I looked around the room and spotted a striking-looking woman with long jet black hair. She was approaching the table, holding hands with a man. That had to be Blaine Masters.

This might be the only chance I had to warn him about the threat to his life, but how could I do that without him thinking I'd lost my mind?

"I thought you weren't going to eat anything tonight," Blaine said, his gaze running over the cake before he looked away.

"I haven't eaten all day just so I could have a piece of cake," the woman said.

"Lila, you'll ruin your figure," Blaine said.

She smacked his arm, a tiny wrinkle marring her otherwise perfect forehead. "I won't ruin my figure. You'll still love me if I eat cake, won't you?"

"Sugar ages the skin," Blaine said.

"One piece of cake won't be a problem." I thrust a large slice of fruit cake into her hands on a white china plate.

"And this cake is mainly fruit, so it's all natural sugars. There's nothing wrong with that."

Blaine grunted as he took a sip of champagne.

"Anything for you, sir?" I asked.

"I don't have a sweet tooth. I don't know why everyone gets so obsessed over cake."

"This is divine." Lila held a piece out to Blaine. "You must try it."

"No thanks," he said. "Look, there's Quentin. I need to talk to him about a business proposal."

I had to say something before I missed my opportunity. "Be careful tonight," I blurted out.

Blaine glanced at me. "Careful about what?"

"Just … be careful. Have fun, but be safe."

He snorted a laugh. "Have you been sneaking the champagne?"

"No! It's just that sometimes people can have a bit too much to drink at events like this."

"Stick to slicing up the cake, serving girl. Don't tell me what to do. Come on, Lila." He took the half-eaten cake out of her hands and set it down before dragging her away.

My heart sank as I watched him go. I'd done what I could to warn him. There was nothing to do other than hope that Lady Philippa's prediction about Blaine Masters was wrong.

Chapter 5

Despite being exhausted from my early start and the stressful day in the kitchen, I couldn't sleep. I tossed and turned for a couple of hours before giving up, making myself a hot chocolate and a plate of delicious buttered toast, and snuggling on my cozy padded window seat at the front of my apartment.

I wrapped a thick, soft throw around my shoulders and curled my knees up to my chest, gazing out the window at the large, dark looming presence of the castle.

Meatball hopped onto the window seat and snuggled by my feet, resting his furry chin on the windowsill so he could look outside.

I balanced my plate of toast on my knees as I slowly ate my way through it.

I was worrying about nothing. There'd been no calls for help or ambulances arriving during the party. And I'd stayed up as late as I could, clearing the kitchen and finding jobs to do so I could listen for any problem.

It was only when Chef Heston forced me out and told me to go home and get some rest that I finally gave in.

But I couldn't rest. From my two brief encounters with Blaine, it was clear that he had a bad attitude. I could easily understand why people didn't like him. But how was he going to die? And when would it happen?

Several lights flicked on in the upper floor rooms of the castle.

I sat up straight and almost lost my plate, grabbing it at the last second so Meatball didn't get his head covered in buttery toast.

More lights flicked on in the castle, and a cold ball of worry grew in my stomach.

I glanced up to Lady Philippa's turret and spotted the glint of her binoculars. She must be watching to see what was going on too. Maybe she'd seen something useful in the grounds. Someone sneaking away after they'd killed Blaine.

I jumped up and headed to the door, then stopped and returned to the window. More lights had come on. "I can't sit here and do nothing, Meatball. That looks like trouble."

"Woof woof." His gaze was on the abandoned toast in my hand.

"It's not wrong to go to the castle and take a quick look. We may be able to help."

"Woof woof!"

"Yes, let's do that." I finished my last slice of toast, fed the crust to Meatball, and hurriedly dressed.

"Woof woof?" Meatball danced around me, excited by the prospect of a late night walk. He raced over, grabbed his leash in his mouth, and presented it to me.

I petted him on the head as I attached his leash, ran a hand through my hair to make myself look presentable, and hurried out the front door with Meatball.

I went through the kitchen entrance, dashing along the corridors until I reached the public rooms of the castle. Before I'd gotten to the great hall, I could hear voices and someone was crying.

"Where's the ambulance?"

My gut clenched as I sped along. An ambulance definitely meant someone had been injured, but was it Blaine?

Alice ran down the main set of stairs, wearing a fluffy blue dressing gown. She spotted me and raced over. "Have you heard the news?"

I winced. "Does it have something to do with Blaine?"

She nodded. "I just found out. He was discovered a few minutes ago at the bottom of the old servants' staircase. He's dead!"

"So, Lady Philippa was right with her prediction about Blaine," I said.

"Granny often is right. Although I discourage her from revealing her predictions to others. It makes people jumpy. I've even heard someone call her a witch. That's just rude."

"I tried to warn Blaine when I saw him at the party. I told him to be careful, but he wouldn't listen to me."

"There was nothing anyone could have done. Blaine Masters only ever listened to himself. No doubt that's how he got to be in this mess. Come on, let's take a look."

I wasn't sure if I wanted to, but I let Alice drag me through the great hall, past the housekeeper's room, and into the west wing. We strode along the gray passageways used by the cleaning staff so they could get around unnoticed by visitors when the castle was open.

There'd be no reason for Blaine to use these stairs, unless he didn't want to be seen.

"I shouldn't be here," I whispered to Alice.

"No one will notice you're here," Alice said. "But if anyone does, I'll say I asked you to come because I was upset about the news. I needed a sympathetic shoulder to lean on. No one will question the word of a princess. If they do, they'll be in trouble."

As we reached the bottom of the back stairs, a security guard hurried away.

I leaned to the left, looking past the small crowd of people who had gathered, and gasped. Blaine was slumped against the wall, his head down. He was dressed only in a pair of red silky boxer shorts.

I looked around the group. Lila was there, along with James. A woman with silky red hair, wearing a dressing gown, clung to his arm, her face pale. There were several more people I didn't recognize.

A large firm hand clamped on my shoulder. "What are you doing here?"

I didn't need to look around to know it was Campbell.

"I insisted Holly come." Alice grabbed my arm and turned us to face him. "I'm in shock over this terrible discovery."

"Perhaps you'd be less shocked if you weren't so close to the body, Princess," Campbell said. "I suggest you go back to your room. The police will be here soon with questions for everyone."

I tore my gaze from the body. "What happened?"

"That's obvious," Campbell said.

"Did he break his neck?" Alice asked.

"The cause of death has yet to be determined, Princess."

Alice bit her lip and looked at me. "What do you think?"

I took a step toward the body. Campbell blocked my path.

"We just want a little peek," Alice said.

"I'm sorry, Princess, but this isn't something you need to see." Campbell arched an eyebrow. "If Holly really is your friend, she'll take you away from here and make sure you're both safe."

Alice huffed out a breath.

"Come on, let's get out of here." It was clear Campbell would do whatever it took to make us leave.

Alice pursed her lips before taking my elbow, and we hurried away. "Blaine was so drunk at the party, it's no wonder he fell down those stairs. I have no idea what he was doing skulking around on the servants' staircase, though."

"Do you really think he just fell?" We reached the south library and checked it was empty before going in.

Alice settled in a seat, and I sat next to her. "Granny didn't say Blaine would be killed. Maybe this was what she meant. A drunken buffoon falling down a set of stone steps and bashing his head."

I twisted my fingers together, my thoughts focused on the image of Blaine on the cold stone floor. "He was on his back."

"Why is that important?"

"Those stairs are narrow. I doubt that if he slipped, he'd have had room to turn around. If you fall face first, you usually try to soften the landing by putting your arms out."

"Which means what?" Alice's nose wrinkled. "Blaine stumbled backward and lost his footing?"

I shook my head. "No, I don't think that's what happened. I didn't get a good look at the back of his head to see if he had any injuries."

Alice pulled a face. "Which we can only be thankful for. There was a blood stain on some stones. He must have hit the back of his head on the way down. I didn't see a cut on the front."

"That's true. And if he did stumble backward and fall, he'd probably have hit the staircase part of the way down. It looked like it was a straight fall. I mean, he didn't stumble, fall, and slide down the stairs."

"Do you think somebody shoved him?" Alice whispered.

"It must have been done with some force to end up in that position," I said.

"What a thought." She shook her head. "Who would do that? And why?"

I shrugged. "I have no idea. I didn't see any injuries on his legs or arms, which suggests there was no struggle before he fell."

"And you would definitely see any cuts or grazes, given how little Blaine was wearing."

"There were scuff marks on his fingertips. Did you see those?"

"No. What does that mean?"

"When you fall, you put your hands out to stop yourself. If he'd been shoved, maybe he put his hands out to try to grab the wall."

"That's so gruesome, Holly. How do you notice things like that?"

"When you're quite done solving this mystery, perhaps you ladies should retire for the night as I suggested." Campbell stood in the doorway, glowering at me.

Alice jumped up. "You must listen to Holly. She's got valuable information about the murder."

"We don't know this was a murder," Campbell said.

"Does anyone know what Blaine was doing on the servants' staircase at this time of night?" I asked.

"I'm sure we'll find out once we've questioned the right people," Campbell said.

"Do you know how long he's been dead?" I asked.

Campbell pressed his lips together and stared me down.

"It's recent," Alice said. "I heard one of the security guards say so. It couldn't have happened more than thirty minutes ago."

"Princess, you must be tired after the party. And you've had a shock. Why don't you go to bed?" Campbell said.

"Oh, no! I can't sleep with something like this going on," Alice said. "I need some air. Holly, you come with me. Keep me company. After all, it's not safe to be on my own if somebody did shove Blaine down the stairs. I could be next."

"Princess, it's best if you don't go spreading rumors until we've ascertained the situation."

"It's not a rumor, it's a prediction. We know the truth." Alice grabbed my hand and tugged me out of the room.

Campbell glared at me until I was out of sight. It was a glare that would make a saint feel guilty. But if Alice wanted me by her side, then that's where I'd be. You didn't say no to Alice Audley.

She dashed through the castle and out the main door, only slowing after she'd sucked in a big breath of air. "What a night."

A sob caught my attention. I turned to see Percy and Lady Diana standing together outside. "Alice, we should go speak to them. They may have a clue about what happened to Blaine."

"Great idea." Alice hurried over with me by her side. "Diana, what a terrible thing to have happened at your party." She wrapped her arms around her before hugging Percy.

Percy ran a hand through his hair several times before sighing. "I told Blaine he was drinking too much tonight. He simply laughed and said I was good for it."

Diana dabbed at her nose with a handkerchief. "What he actually said was that you'd married up, and you should take full advantage of your strategic marriage into the Audley family." Her gaze went to the castle. "It was a mistake to invite him."

"You said we couldn't exclude anybody. Everyone who came to our wedding had to receive a party invite," Percy said. "I suggested we leave Blaine off the list, but you wouldn't hear of it."

She lifted a hand. "I didn't think this would happen. Blaine's usually fun at parties. And he used to throw his own amazing gatherings. People would talk about them for weeks after they'd happened."

Alice leaned closer to me. "I heard that Blaine held those parties so he could find new girlfriends. It was always eighty percent gorgeous women and twenty percent guys, so he could have his pick."

Percy chuckled softly. "That was Blaine through and through. He was always looking for the good time. His motto was that it's better to burn out than fade away. What a way to go though."

"Does anyone know why he was on those stairs?" I asked.

Lady Diana's forehead wrinkled. "No. What are you doing here? Aren't you the cake lady?"

"The cake lady is my friend," Alice said. "I trust Holly with my life. She's always there for me, and she makes the best brownies in the world. I asked her to be here."

Lady Diana shrugged before looking away. "I'm surprised Blaine knew about that staircase. Maybe he got lost. Perhaps he was drunk and went for a walk to clear his head."

"He went for a walk in his underpants?" Alice said. "It's chilly in the castle, even during the summer months."

"It has to be something to do with a woman," Percy said. "Blaine still had a lot of growing up to do. He thought being a ladies' man was cool. And although he brought Lila to this party, I know he was dating several other women."

"How do you know that?" Lady Diana asked. "You haven't been covering for him again, have you?"

Percy shot her a guilty look. "He's my friend. He tells me things."

"I hope you've not been gossiping about our marriage to him."

"You know Blaine, he only ever liked to talk about himself." Percy shook his head. "I still can't believe what's happened."

The wail of an ambulance siren filtered through the air.

"We'd better get back inside," Percy said. "Come on, Diana."

She caught hold of his elbow, and after a nod goodbye, they left us on our own.

"What are you going to do?" Alice turned to me and gripped my shoulders.

"What do you mean? I can't do anything."

"You have to. You should look into this. Somebody pushed Blaine down those stairs. Maybe it was one of the women he was seeing."

"He wouldn't have met someone at the party and tried to get together with them tonight," I said. "Not when he had a date with him."

"Of course he would. Have you met his personal assistant? She's also here." Alice used air quotes as she said *personal assistant*. "She is va va voom out of this world stunning. If I was Blaine's girlfriend, I'd keep a very close eye on her. What's to say he wasn't in a relationship with his assistant behind his girlfriend's back? It would have been such a Blaine thing to do."

"It doesn't make sense that he'd bring his assistant to a party."

"It does if she assists him with everything in his life." Alice waggled her eyebrows. "Sabine goes everywhere with him, apparently. I overheard Lila muttering about it to somebody at the party. She wasn't happy."

"I shouldn't get involved in this," I said. "Campbell wasn't happy that I was at the crime scene."

"What if the police don't see what you do? They might call this an accident, and a murderer could get away, although I'm not sad that Blaine won't be around anymore. I didn't like him."

I nodded. He seemed to have that effect on a lot of people. But he was dead. What if I turned my back and something bad had happened to him? Did anyone deserve such an undignified death? Discovered wearing nothing but a pair of underpants. Even if they were very nice underpants.

"You must look into this." Alice shook my arms. "Ask a few questions. I can help. I'm great at getting people to open up to me. People are never careful about what they say in front of me because they think I'm stupid."

"No! Alice, you're not stupid. You're amazing."

She grinned. "We both know that, but it does no harm to make people believe I'm away with the fairies most of the time."

"Let's take a step back for now," I said. "Campbell and his team are on the case, and the police will be here soon. I'm sure that once they've processed the scene, they'll come up with the same conclusions as we have."

Alice's bottom lip trembled. "Someone killed Blaine inside the castle. This is my home. I can't let them get away with that."

"We won't. I promise." I looked back at the castle. Whatever had happened to Blaine, it definitely wasn't an accident. I just had to hope that Campbell and the police saw that too.

Chapter 6

Meatball's warm, damp nose roused me from my restless slumber.

I yawned and slung my arm over his back before giving him a hearty rub. "I hope you slept better than I did."

"Woof."

It seemed we'd both had bad nights. I glanced at the clock to see it was just before seven in the morning. I'd only managed a few hours of sleep. Every time I'd shut my eyes, I kept thinking about what I'd seen at the foot of the servants' stairs.

After another long, loud yawn, and a belly rub for Meatball, I rolled out of bed, took a shower, and then dressed.

Meatball bounced in front of me as I headed to my small kitchen and pulled out the breakfast things.

"I'm thinking this is a crime of passion," I said to him. "Everyone I spoke to about Blaine said he was a cheat and couldn't be trusted around women. He must have pushed one of his girlfriends too far, and she literally pushed him down the stairs."

"Woof woof." Meatball wagged his tail.

"I'm glad you agree. Which means we're looking for a woman with a tight connection to Blaine. Someone he was in a relationship with. Well, if you can call what he did with his girlfriends' real relationships."

Meatball nosed his empty food dish toward me.

"I'm on it. Breakfast is almost served." I refilled his water bowl and set it down before pulling out his dog kibble and scooping out a serving.

Meatball set about his food, noisily chomping as I made a pot of tea and toasted a poppy seed bagel.

"There's the obvious suspect, the current girlfriend," I said. "Lila. I don't know much about her, but she's stunning. Most likely a model. And then there's Sabine, the personal assistant. She also needs looking into."

Meatball's mouth was full of kibble so he didn't respond, but he gave a wag of his tail as if he was still paying attention and agreeing with everything I said.

"And then there's Lady Diana." I didn't like to have her on my suspect list, but she'd made it clear she didn't think much of Blaine. Had he done something to offend her at the party?

I was munching on my last piece of bagel when a message pinged on my phone. I opened it to see it was from Alice.

Meet me in the dining parlor ASAP!

I hit reply. *What's going on?*

Hurry! It's an emergency!

I stuffed down my last piece of bagel, ran my hands through my still damp hair, and grabbed my shoes. "Come on, Meatball. Alice needs our help."

Having munched down the last of his kibble, he trotted to the door. I attached his leash and headed out. I hoped everything was okay with Alice. It was unlike her to message me so early. She enjoyed a lie-in. I didn't imagine I'd see anyone from the family much before noon.

I slid through a side door in the south wing and into the castle with Meatball. I hurried along the corridor, nodding and saying good morning to the cleaning staff as I passed them.

The door to the dining parlor was open when I arrived. I poked my head around the side.

Alice sat at a table, along with Rupert, Lady Diana, and Percy.

She looked over and grinned. "There you are. I was thinking you weren't going to make it before I ate all the pain au chocolat."

Rupert stood as I approached. "Good morning, Holly. It's nice to see you."

I stopped by the table and smiled at him before turning my attention to Alice. "What's the emergency?"

"The emergency is that I'm eating delicious breakfast pastries, and I didn't want you to miss out." She inclined her head and widened her eyes before shooting a glance at Lady Diana and Percy.

I stifled a groan. This was a setup. She'd brought me here so I could do more digging into what happened to Blaine. "I should leave you to it. I don't want to interrupt a family breakfast."

"I insist you join us. You're here now." Alice jumped up, grabbed my hand, and dragged me to a seat. "And I've got special treats for Meatball. Don't be cruel and deprive him of his treats. You love treats, don't you?" She patted her knee.

Meatball bounced on his hind legs and waggled his front paws in the air.

Alice laughed. "He's such a good dog. Rupert, insist Holly has breakfast with us."

Rupert dabbed a white linen napkin against his mouth before pulling out a chair for me. "Absolutely! There's plenty to go around. Do join us."

Percy smiled at me and nodded, while Lady Diana barely paid me any attention, her fingers tapping on the top of the table, her fruit salad untouched.

"Only if it's no trouble me being here," I said.

Rupert slid my chair in as I sat. "Alice always goes over the top when she has her continental breakfasts. There's enough food to feed a dozen people."

"Not when you're around." Alice returned to her seat. "You always eat more croissants than me. I have to order extra in case you steal what I want."

"You always make out that I'm so greedy." Rupert settled in his seat and set to work on his croissant.

"That's because we've grown up together. I know what a greedy guts you are," Alice said.

Meatball bounded around the table a few times, sniffing everyone and searching for crumbs on the floor.

"Oh! I almost forgot you." Alice took a packet out of her purse on the back of her chair. "These are game and spinach chews. Apparently, it's important that dogs get their greens. I got these from Granny. Now, be a good boy and sit."

Meatball stopped bounding around and sat by Alice's chair, his eyes big and pleading.

She giggled as she handed him the treat.

He wagged his tail before settling on the carpet to enjoy it.

"We were just talking about what happened last night," Alice said.

"When I woke this morning, I hoped it had been a nightmare," Percy said.

"If only that were true," Lady Diana said. "That's all people will talk about. They won't remember the fact it was our five year wedding anniversary. Blaine always was selfish. He stole the limelight whenever he could."

"Getting murdered will definitely steal the limelight," I said.

Lady Diana blinked at me as if it was the first time she'd noticed me in the room. "Indeed it would. So typical of Blaine."

"I expect he'd much rather be alive than the source of gossip," Rupert said.

"Has there been any progress in discovering what happened to him?" I asked.

"Campbell's leading on the case," Alice said. "He's already questioned a number of people."

"The trouble is, there were over three hundred guests at the party last night," Rupert said.

"Three hundred and twenty-two," Lady Diana said. "All our close friends and family."

I glanced at her. I could count my close friends on one hand. How could anyone be so popular?

Rupert nodded. "It'll take Campbell and his team a while to question everyone."

"You must be able to discount most of the guests," I said. "If they didn't know Blaine or have solid alibis, they won't be suspects."

"Suspects? What are you talking about?" Lady Diana said. "This was an accident."

I bit my bottom lip and glanced at Alice. "I'm not so sure it was."

Percy cleared his throat. "I didn't want to alarm you, my dear. The security chaps do think foul play was involved. They're collecting evidence, but when I spoke to the castle's head of security, he mentioned an ongoing investigation. That suggests that this wasn't an accident."

"Murder! At our party! Could this get any worse?" Lady Diana massaged her forehead with her fingers.

"Have the police questioned you about where you both were?" I asked.

"We were in our room, of course," Lady Diana said. "I was exhausted after the party. As soon as my head hit the pillow, I went straight to sleep."

Percy glanced at his wife before nodding. "That's right. We were both asleep. We got woken to the sound of people shouting for help."

"Which room was Blaine staying in?" I asked.

"He was across from you two." Alice pointed at Lady Diana.

"Did either of you hear him leave his room last night?" I asked.

"Nothing disturbs me once I'm asleep," Lady Diana said. "Percy had to shake me to wake me up and let me know what was happening."

Percy shifted in his seat and nodded again.

"I can't figure how this could be murder," Lady Diana said. "Blaine was drunk. He simply fell."

Alice raised her eyebrows and nodded at me.

I still wasn't sure about asking more questions about this murder. Campbell would kill me if he found out what I was doing. But I hadn't set up this impromptu breakfast interrogation. This was Alice's doing. I could imagine Campbell wouldn't see it that way.

"If anyone wanted Blaine dead, it would have been one of his women," Percy said. "Although he was dating Lila Mendelsham, and she's a lovely girl, he mentioned that he wanted to upgrade his model."

"That's just disrespectful," Alice said.

"That's Blaine," Lady Diana said. "Or rather, it was. He was never happy with what he had. He always thought the grass was greener. The thing about grass is that if you don't tend to it, water it, and pay it attention, it dies. Blaine was always looking for the easy option. The new, exciting relationship."

Percy lifted his phone from the table as it buzzed. "I do apologize. I don't usually have my phone at the table, but I'm expecting a call from Japan. I need to take this. It's work. Do excuse me." He pushed back his chair and headed out of the room, his phone to his ear.

Lady Diana tapped the back of Alice's hand. "I shouldn't say this, but I'm not sad that Blaine is no longer around. I was getting concerned about his friendship with Percy."

"Why? What were they doing together that had you worried?" Alice asked.

"Blaine was always trying to lead Percy astray. Blaine didn't believe in monogamy. He thought it wasn't a natural state for a man. I know that he tempted Percy on numerous occasions with beautiful women."

"Oh! You're talking about those tabloid pictures that came out a few months ago. I've seen the ones of Percy getting a lap dance." Alice giggled. "The woman had very large ... assets. She pressed them into his face. He was lucky not to be smothered."

"Yes! Thank you. I don't need to be reminded of that humiliation." Lady Diana stabbed a spoon into her fruit salad. "Everyone has seen those pictures."

"I haven't," I said.

"Percy was innocent. Those pictures were all Blaine's fault," Lady Diana said. "I tried to stop Percy from being friends with Blaine, but he insisted the friendship remain intact."

"You don't think Blaine ever succeeded in making Percy stray?" Alice asked.

I sucked in a breath as I waited for the answer. That wasn't a bad motive for murder. Blaine knew a secret about Percy. Could he have been threatening to reveal it and ruin his marriage? Did Percy shove Blaine down the stairs to keep him quiet?

"I trust Percy." Lady Diana's hand shook as she took a sip of tea.

"Then you have nothing to worry about," Alice said. She bit a large chunk off her pain au chocolat.

"Of course not. Our marriage is perfect." Lady Diana played with the napkin on her lap as her hand fluttered against her chest.

She wasn't behaving as if she was in a perfect marriage. Maybe there was a problem between her and Percy. Percy could have given into temptation if Blaine was constantly throwing women at him. Or maybe it was the other way around. Perhaps Blaine had tempted Lady Diana to stray with him. Whatever was going on between the two of them, something was wrong with that relationship.

Lady Diana glanced at the door. "I always tell Percy not to conduct his business over meals. I'd better go and find him. I'll catch up with you later, Alice." She nodded at Rupert, completely ignored me, and left the room.

"So, what do you think, Holly?" Alice leaned toward me. "Could they be suspects?"

"I don't know enough about them to make a judgment just yet. Percy looks shaken up about it, though."

"Diana isn't sad," Alice said. "She was almost dancing in her seat. She must be delighted that a thorn in her side has been yanked out. Blaine's gone, and her husband will no longer be tempted by beautiful women."

"You can't think either of them killed Blaine," Rupert said.

"Percy has known Blaine for years. They could have fallen out over something. Women, business, money. Anything's possible," Alice said.

"Blackmail," I said.

Alice clapped her hands together. "I knew it! You can't resist this mystery. Why do you think it might be blackmail?"

"I don't. Not for certain." I bit my bottom lip, not sure whether to share my unfounded idea. "Was Percy convincing when he said where he was at the time Blaine was pushed down the stairs? He seemed shifty to me."

"You don't think he was in bed with Diana?" Alice asked. "Where was he?"

"I don't know. But if Lady Diana had been asleep, Percy could have slipped out of the room. She said she was a sound sleeper."

"Percy's a good guy," Rupert said. "I don't think he had any problems with Blaine. Certainly nothing that was worth killing over."

"Unless Blaine had a secret about Percy that he was threatening to reveal," Alice said.

I nodded. "Maybe Percy slipped up with one of these women. Blaine decided to use that to his advantage."

"That's too crass, even for Blaine," Rupert said. "Besides, he's got money."

"What about Lady Diana?" I asked. "Blaine was a good-looking guy."

"You thought he was good-looking?" Rupert's brow lowered.

Alice slapped his hand. "Everyone could see that Blaine was a gorgeous guy. That doesn't make him a nice person. And that doesn't mean Holly had plans to marry him."

"Ah! Of course. That's not what I meant." Rupert busied himself by spreading strawberry preserves on his croissant.

I bit the inside of my mouth to stop from smiling. "What I was getting at, was that maybe it wasn't Percy who strayed. Could Lady Diana and Blaine have had an encounter?"

Alice's hand flew to her mouth. "She hated him. She only invited him to the party so she could recreate her wedding. Diana wouldn't have touched Blaine Masters with someone else's ten-foot barge pole. No, it can't be that."

I shrugged as I helped myself to a pain au chocolat. "It's just ideas at this stage."

"This is so exciting. Holly, you must get involved with figuring this out," Alice said. "You're so good at thinking outside the box. I bet Campbell and his team haven't even thought about Blaine being with Diana. What a hoot if it was true. She always bleats on about her perfect marriage and how she's married to the most wonderful man. Her life is perfection."

"Nobody's life is perfection," I said.

"I know that. I'm having to endure weekly dance lessons because of the awful upcoming ball season. It's a torture."

"It sounds dreadful."

She giggled. "Diana is a big show off. She always has been, ever since she was a child. She'd hate it if any rumors came out that she'd been intimate with Blaine."

"Don't start those rumors," I said. "I've got no proof that they were involved. I'm just suggesting theories about who may have had a motive for killing Blaine."

"It's an excellent theory," Alice said. "I insist that you investigate this mystery. This murder happened in our home. We can't let that go unanswered."

"I'm sure Campbell will make sure it's answered," I said.

"By hushing everything up and making out it's an accident," Alice said.

"He'll do a solid job," Rupert said. "We can trust Campbell and his team to do the right thing."

"I agree," I said. "I'm taking a step back from this one."

"Holly ... Oh! Do you have a middle name?" Alice asked.

"Sure. It's Rosemary."

Alice jabbed a finger at me. "Holly Rosemary Holmes. You must investigate this murder. You know what I do to people who don't follow my orders."

I grinned and exchanged a glance with Rupert. "You threaten to have them beheaded?"

"Exactly. I can help out if you need to talk to any of the suspects. I know everyone. We can fix things up, just like I did this morning with Diana and Percy. This was a perfect setting. Everyone was relaxed, happy, and eating. No one thought it was odd that you were asking questions about murder."

"You were asking most of the questions," I said.

"This will be easy. We'll put together a list of suspects and work our way through it. We'll be discreet. Campbell won't need to know. And if you're really quick, we might beat him in finding out who did it. That would put a smile on his face."

"I doubt that very much. And as for threatening to behead me if I don't get involved, Campbell will do that anyway if he finds out what we're up to."

"He's a big pussycat. If he causes you any trouble, you come and see me."

I sighed as I took a bite of my warm pain au chocolat. I was intrigued about what had happened to Blaine. Maybe one or two discreet questions wouldn't do any harm.

"If we're going to investigate, we need to be inconspicuous," I said. "Campbell has warned me off before about poking around in things that are none of my business."

Alice shook her head. "I bet he'll say something like 'murder's not a laughing matter. Your place is in the kitchen. Keep your nose out.'"

I snorted a laugh. "That's a good impression."

"So, are you going to get investigating?" Alice asked.

I nodded. "I'll put my thinking cap on at work today. But I'm promising nothing. If Campbell tells me to keep away, that's what I'll do."

"Hasn't he told you to keep your nose out before?" Alice said. "Did you listen to him then?"

My cheeks grew warm. "That was different."

"And this is different too," Alice said. "Holly Holmes, we're going to solve this murder."

Chapter 7

"Butter for greasing, self-rising flour, caster sugar, two eggs, mixed spice, and vanilla extract." I tapped my chin with a finger. "Icing sugar." I hefted a bag out and placed it on the counter.

This was my fifth attempt at making spice and vanilla jumbles from a Tudor recipe I'd found in an old book in the family library. So far, I hadn't succeeded in making anything I was willing to share.

Maybe I was using the wrong kind of flour. What we had in the kitchen was different to the flour used five hundred years ago. I just couldn't get the consistency right. The jumbles were either too soggy in the middle, the edges burnt, or they went flat. I hadn't nailed this recipe yet, but I was determined to keep trying. I had just enough time for one more go before I took my lunch break.

"Everybody gather around." Chef Heston wheeled a trolley into the center of the kitchen, the remains of the sky rise cake laid out on plates.

A dozen kitchen staff collected around him and accepted slices of the cake.

This was unusual behavior for Chef Heston. He never brought us together for a cake break. What was he up to?

"It's a shame to see this go to waste." He looked around the gathered group.

"I couldn't agree more," Louise said. "It's amazing cake."

I nodded at her and smiled as she tucked into a piece of cherry sponge I'd made.

"However, we're not just here to eat leftover cake," Chef Heston said. "We can learn a valuable lesson from what happened recently. Lorcan Blaze is one of the best. He runs a Michelin starred restaurant and has over twenty successful patisseries across the world. Everyone who samples his desserts raves about his food and what a genius he is. But even a genius can make a mistake. Food poisoning is a serious business. It's been known to kill people."

Sally nudged me. "We're always careful here. Our kitchen is pristine."

I nodded. We prided ourselves on high standards.

"I'm certain that Lorcan didn't get food poisoning while he was here. Apparently, he was dining at a restaurant in London two nights before he arrived. Several of the other customers have also become ill. There was a problem with the chicken liver pâté." Chef Heston shook his head. "We all know that we need to be careful with food like that. Let this be a warning to everyone. It happened to Lorcan, so it can happen to you. Hygiene standards are there for a reason. If I catch anyone slacking off and forgetting what those standards are, they'll be fired without question. Nobody gets sick from my kitchen. Is that understood?"

Everyone nodded and murmured their agreement.

"Good work, people. Let's keep the excellent standards we already have. Finish your cake and get back to work." Chef Heston grabbed a slice of cake before striding away.

"Do you know how Lorcan's doing?" I asked Sally.

"He's still sick as a dog," she said. "They've put him in a guest room as far away from everyone else as possible. He's causing a right stink and demanding feather pillows and extra blankets. The man sounds like a nightmare."

"Holly, have you finished your cake?" Chef Heston said from across the kitchen.

I crammed the last mouthful of lemon sponge into my mouth before nodding.

"Good. Take this toast up to Lorcan." Chef Heston handed me a tray.

I looked down at the tray, my stomach clenching. He was the last person I wanted to see. "I've still got work to do here."

"No, you haven't. I've seen that you've checked everything off your to-do list on the board. Besides, Lorcan wants to talk to you about the cake."

My shoulders tightened. "Is he unhappy about something?"

"That's for you to find out. He's seen some pictures of what we made and wants to discuss them with you."

I adjusted my grip on the tray. There was no way I could get out of this, no matter what I said. The cake we'd made was amazing. I knew that. But going to face the music in front of a sick, petulant baker who had an ego the size of this castle was something I wasn't looking forward to.

"Get a move on." Chef Heston gave me a gentle nudge toward the door. "He's on the second floor, past the old nursery and last door on the left. I'm sure you'll hear him before you get to the room. Apparently, he shouts a lot if he doesn't get his own way."

"I know somebody else like that."

"Sorry? I didn't catch that." Chef Heston's eyes narrowed.

"Nothing, Chef. I'll get right on it." I bumped the door open with my hip and hurried to the main staircase. I dashed up it and walked along the corridor until I found Lorcan's room. I knocked and waited.

"Enter," Lorcan said.

I entered the room and found chaos. Blankets were tossed to the floor, several pillows had been thrown against the wall, and there were numerous half-empty glasses of water on the nightstand beside a large four poster bed.

Lorcan scowled at me. "At last! I've been wanting to see you all day. Why didn't you come as soon as I demanded?" He sat up in the bed, his hair a crumpled greasy mess and his skin tainted gray.

"I only just learned you wanted to see me."

He sank into the bed and groaned.

"How are you feeling?" I asked.

"I'm dying."

"Food poisoning can make you feel bad," I said. "Have you had anything to eat?"

"I'm too weak to eat."

"It might make you feel better," I said. "If whatever made you sick has left your body, you'll need nourishment."

"Oh, it has. I was violently ill all night." He flung an arm over his eyes. "Not that anyone cares."

I glanced at the closed bathroom door, pitying the cleaner who'd have to attend to that mess. "A bit of plain food could settle your stomach. I've got some toast."

He groaned and sank further into the bed. "I don't have the energy to lift it to my mouth."

"I'll leave it on the floor by the side of the bed. Maybe you can try later."

"I won't be able to reach it from there. Feed me," he said.

My head jerked back, and I stared at him. "You want me to hand feed you toast?"

"Break it into tiny pieces and put it in my mouth. I have barely enough energy to speak. And there's a lot I want to say to you."

He looked really unwell, but there was no way I was going to feed him.

Lorcan moaned. "Help me. I may not last the day."

I repressed a sigh. Why did most men act like feeble idiots when they became unwell? Rather than leaving him in his pathetic hour of need, I compromised. I took the toast off the tray and sat on the edge of his bed before placing a slice in his hand. "Try feeding yourself. If you can do it, you'll feel like you've achieved something."

His lips pressed together as he lowered his hand and looked at the toast. "This is brown bread. I only eat white toast."

I forced a smile. "Try it, anyway. It's home-made in the kitchen. You might like it."

He took a tiny bite before dropping the toast on his chest. "That's your fault. I told you I was too weak to feed myself. I'll starve, and you don't care."

I grabbed the toast and placed it back on the plate. "Is there anything else I can do for you?" Maybe put him out of his misery if he kept being so difficult?

Lorcan's eyes narrowed before he nodded. "You were involved with finishing the cake for the anniversary party?"

"I was. Chef Heston had me up at dawn to make sure we didn't let Lady Diana down."

"Hmm. I've seen pictures. It looked uneven."

"No. Everything was measured, and we followed your exact recipe. The levels were perfectly even." I wasn't letting him criticize the work that had gone into saving his neck.

"The coloring was wrong, and you made the gold dots on the middle layer too big."

"No, I didn't. They were two-and-a-half centimeters as per the instructions."

He grunted. "They looked big in the pictures."

"If they were too big it was because your instructions were incorrect."

Lorcan sucked in a breath. "My instructions are never wrong. How dare you."

I stood from the bed and placed my hands on my hips. I needed to be careful, or I'd start yelling. "How dare I? You come into our kitchen, barking orders and being rude to everyone. And the first time I met you, you could see I needed help, and you abandoned me. You took over my food preparation area in the kitchen, then you had the cheek to get sick. I saved your neck. We pulled together in the kitchen to make sure everything ran smoothly and the anniversary party went without a hitch. I worked my backside off to make sure Lady Diana and Percy got the cake of their dreams."

He spluttered several words, but I lifted a finger.

"I'm not finished. You've been rude to me ever since we met. You challenged me over my food, yet I proved that I know how to bake. Now you're being rude about the cake I made to save your hide. You should be grateful. I didn't have to do it. I could have stayed in bed and not helped."

"I … I … don't believe you've just said that. You think you can—"

"I'm an excellent baker. I make amazing cakes, and I'm proud of that. If you have a problem with me being your competition when it comes to making delicious desserts, you deal with it. I'm not sitting here feeding you toast and stroking your ego. You're not a nice man, Lorcan Blaze." I gasped out a breath, my hands tingling. I couldn't believe what I'd done. This was going to get me in so much trouble. I turned and headed to the door before I said anything else.

"Wait a moment."

My hand was already on the doorknob. "What is it?"

"You have spirit, kitchen girl."

I turned back to him. "My name is Holly Holmes."

His gaze ran over me. "Holly, I admire your ambition. Where do you see yourself in five years' time?"

I squinted at him. "Why do you care?"

"Because you intrigue me. I'm not an easy man to work with, but that's because I set my standards so high."

"So I've heard," I said.

"I make no apologies for that. I wouldn't be where I am now if I didn't expect excellence from everyone I worked with. It's rare that I find a new face to fit my team. Most people don't have what it takes to join me. When you join the big leagues, it changes your life."

"I'm sure your staff are delighted that they get to work with you every day. It must be a joy."

He snorted a laugh. "They get extremely well paid. And when they do leave me, they can step into whatever job they desire. Working for Lorcan Blaze guarantees you a golden future. So, Holly Holmes, what do you say?"

"About what?"

"Stepping into the big leagues. If you like change and a challenge, why don't you give me a call?"

My mouth dropped open, and I leaned against the door. "You're offering me a job?"

"It doesn't happen often. Most people I meet fall short of my expectations. Maybe your cake last night was a little wonky—"

"It wasn't wonky." I lifted my chin and stared him down. "It was perfection."

His grin looked shark like. "It was close to perfection. You still have things to learn. Come work for me. I'll change your life."

Words escaped me. I'd just insulted him and told him I'd saved his backside, and he was offering me a chance to work for him.

"I understand. I usually get this reaction when someone receives such an incredible offer."

"I mean. I don't … are you serious?"

"I'm always serious when it comes to my food. I make excellence, I expect excellence, and I only want excellent people around me. Take this." He lifted his wallet from the nightstand, pulled out a card, and held it out.

I walked back to the bed, my knees shaky, and took the card.

"Few people have my personal contact information. You're now one of the privileged few. The package I offer all employees is top class. You'll learn a host of new skills, and you'll get to travel the world thanks to me. I'll expect to hear from you soon."

I swallowed and tucked the card into my pocket. "I'm not sure about this. I'm happy here."

He dismissed the comment with a jerk of his fingers. "Happy, content, and not challenged. There's a lot more I could get out of you if you're up to it."

I backed away and reached the door. "I'll think about it."

"Don't think too long."

I turned and hurried out of the bedroom, my mind whirling. That was the last thing I'd expected. Lorcan's reputation was outstanding. This could be an incredible opportunity. But I didn't want to leave Audley Castle. I loved my job. I loved all the people here. I didn't even mind the ghostly whispers and cold spots. They were what made this place unique.

I slowed as I passed an open window. Raised voices filtered up to me. I peered out the window to see two women standing toe to toe arguing.

One was Lila Mendelsham, but I didn't recognize the redhead. Whatever was going on between them looked intense.

I put all thoughts of Lorcan's job offer to the back of my mind as I hurried down the stairs. Could this argument be about Blaine?

There was only one way to find out.

Chapter 8

As I stepped out the side entrance onto the gravel driveway, the woman with the red hair pushed Lila. She staggered back on her high heels before letting out a screech.

The other woman turned on her equally high heels and stalked away.

"This isn't over," Lila yelled. "I'll get you for this."

"Is everything okay?" I hurried over to her.

"No! Nothing is okay. That … that creature shouldn't even be here." Lila pulled her long hair off her face, two red dots of color on her cheeks.

"I recognize you from the party," I said.

She glanced at me, and her nose wrinkled. "You were at the party?"

"Not in an official capacity," I said. "I brought in the anniversary cake."

Lila's eyes brightened for a second. "That was an awesome cake. I didn't get to have much of it, though. Blaine never liked me eating sugar."

"That's not a problem you have to worry about now."

Her large almond-shaped eyes narrowed. "Did you know him? You weren't another one of his …" She waved a hand in the direction the other woman had gone.

"No! Nothing like that. But I heard what happened to him."

"Everyone has." Lila tipped her head back and blew out a breath. "This is all such a mess. And people like Sabine are only making it worse. This has nothing to do with her. She was an employee of Blaine's. I don't even know why she's still hanging around. Most likely looking for her next victim to dig her claws into. What better place than a castle full of rich people to find your next sucker?"

So, the argument was about Blaine. This conversation just got interesting.

"You look like you need a break," I said. "I can make us coffee and cake if you need five minutes. It's never fun to fight with someone."

She sighed and shook her head. "I don't do carbs on a week day."

"Try a small piece. Cake always settles my nerves when I'm angry about something."

Lila tilted her head. "Have you got any of the anniversary cake left?"

"That's all gone. But I can offer you brownies, Victoria sponge, lemon drizzle cake, strawberry scones. Whatever you want." And if I could get some time alone with Lila, I could find out more about her relationship with Blaine and her fight with Sabine.

Her tongue traced across her bottom lip. "Bring out a selection. I may be able to manage a few bites of something."

"Right this way. We have a bench outside the kitchen which we use when we're on breaks. Wait here. I'll be back in a minute." I dashed into the kitchen, grabbed the cakes, mugs, and coffee, and headed back, relieved to see Lila sitting on the bench.

I set the cake laden tray down and settled opposite her.

Without waiting for me to hand out the cakes, Lila grabbed the biggest chocolate brownie and took a huge bite.

I passed her a mug of coffee, then selected a strawberry scone for myself.

"Oh my goodness, this is amazing." Lila ate the chocolate brownie in three bites before licking crumbs off her fingers.

"There are plenty more in the kitchen if you love brownies."

Lila shook her head. "No, I really don't do carbs." She snatched up the lemon drizzle cake and took a bite.

I bit my bottom lip to stop from smiling. "I always find comfort in cake, especially during stressful times. I imagine you're stressed about what happened with Blaine."

She finished the lemon drizzle cake before nodding. "It was horrible. I woke to find the bed empty. Usually, Blaine wakes me with his snoring when he's had a heavy night of drinking. I turned over, and his side was still warm, but he wasn't there. He must have just left the bed."

"Did you go looking for him?"

"No. I was dozing off when I heard people shouting. I was annoyed at first. I don't like being disturbed. I got up to tell them to be quiet, when I heard someone shout Blaine's name and to get an ambulance. That's when I panicked." She took the slice of Victoria sponge and bit into it.

"Who discovered Blaine at the bottom of the stairs?" I asked.

Lila's eyes narrowed. "Apparently, it was a security guard on patrol. But Sabine was one of the first on the scene after it happened."

"That must have been upsetting for her."

"If she had real emotions, it would have been. I don't believe a word that comes out of that harlot's mouth. Everyone knew she was a lot more than Blaine's personal assistant. She can't even type properly. Those long false nails of hers get in the way."

"So, why did Blaine employ her?"

She huffed out a breath. "One guess."

"Do you think Blaine was cheating on you?"

"Sadly, yes. The most humiliating thing was that he wasn't even discreet about it. He used to brag to his friends. He was disgusting."

I sipped my coffee. "If you don't mind me saying, why stay with a man who's unfaithful to you?"

Lila finished the Victoria sponge cake. "Blaine still had some growing up to do. It sometimes meant he made poor life choices."

"He must have been in his mid-thirties," I said. "When exactly was he planning on growing up?"

She smirked. "Good point. It would have happened eventually. All his friends were the same. They played the field and didn't like to be 'tied down', as they called it, to any one girl. And there's so much temptation out there. When you're rich and handsome, all the women chase after you. I had the option of giving up on my dream to be married to Blaine or grit my teeth and see it through to the end."

"The end? What did the end mean for you?"

"Marriage! We were serious about each other," she said. "One day, he'd have opened his eyes and realized how amazing I am. The marriage proposal would have followed. And I was working on that, getting him to see we were a perfect match. If I invested the time now to fix him, he'd have been the ideal husband. Now, all my hard work has gone to waste."

That sounded like the worst plan for a happy marriage. You shouldn't go into a relationship in the hope of altering a person. Sure, a few tweaks around the edges were fine, but changing a person's nature would never work. Blaine sounded like a cheat through and through. If he'd lived, he'd probably still have been having affairs when he was in his eighties.

"You mentioned Blaine was in a relationship with Sabine. That must have been hard for you to deal with."

"If you can call it a relationship." Lila scowled at her piece of cake. "Sabine is so smug about it. And she's acting more upset than I am about Blaine's death. Trust me, it's all an act."

There was a suspicious lack of tears coming from Lila considering her boyfriend, and future husband, was dead.

"She did see the body," I said. "That's got to have shocked her."

Lila pursed her lips. "So did I. And he was my boyfriend."

"Was Sabine the only other woman Blaine was seeing?"

Lila waved a hand in the air. "I very much doubt it. She was one of his regulars, though. They've been 'working' together for six months. I tried to prevent him from hiring her, but he said she had just the right assets." Her top lip curled. "I knew exactly what he meant. I figured I'd give him a couple of months of fun and he'd tire of her. She's so obvious in her high heels and enhanced cleavage. But then the relationship carried on and they became serious. I almost didn't come to this party when Blaine said he'd arranged for Sabine to be here."

"Did you confront Blaine? Tell him it wasn't on to see you and Sabine at the same time?"

She arched an eyebrow. "You clearly don't know much about men. That would never have worked. What if Blaine chose her over me? Besides, their relationship would have played itself out. Blaine would have come back to me, and Sabine would have been a distant and unpleasant memory for both of us."

I resisted the desire to shudder. That sounded like a match made in hell. "Has anyone spoken to you about the possibility Blaine's fall wasn't an accident?"

Lila nodded. "Are you going to eat that scone?"

I pushed it toward her. If cake kept Lila talking, I'd give her whatever she wanted. "It's all yours."

"Thanks. It looks yummy."

"You don't seem surprised about Blaine's death not being an accident."

She shrugged. "I'm not. Blaine always said what was on his mind, even if it offended somebody. He didn't care about other people's feelings. He was always about himself and what he could get out of life. I told the security man who spoke to me that they'd have a job finding whoever shoved him down those stairs. One thing I did make clear though was that it wasn't me. I was asleep in my room. I'm sure someone saw me coming out of the bedroom when it all kicked off."

"Can you think of anybody here who might have wanted to kill Blaine?"

She tapped her pink painted nails on the table. "That's a tricky one. He annoyed a lot of people, but I did see him arguing with James Postle before the party."

"What were they arguing about?"

"I didn't hear. I was too far away. They were standing close, and it looked full-on. James was the one to walk away, and he didn't look happy when he did. His shoulders were hunched, and he had his hands clenched into fists."

This was surprising news. When I'd met James, he'd seemed like a nice guy. What had Blaine done to anger him?

Lila sat back and patted her stomach. "I have such a carb food baby going on. I need to go for a long run to burn this off."

"I'm sorry about what happened to Blaine," I said. "But trust me, there are loads of great guys out there. Maybe ones who won't cheat on you. You shouldn't wait for a guy to change before he realizes how amazing you are. Find someone who wants to look after you and no one else."

Lila shook her head as she stood. "You're a sweet thing, but you have no idea how men's minds work. I knew what I was getting into when it came to Blaine. And sure, I wish he hadn't cheated on me, but that's how things are in my social circle. You have to look right, keep your mouth shut, and eventually, you bag the rich guy. I almost envy you, a simple life, making cakes every day, not understanding how the world works."

I blinked at her. "I know how the world works just fine."

She patted my hand. "Great cakes. Stick to that, not giving relationship advice." Lila walked away, one hand cradling her swollen stomach.

My forehead wrinkled as I ran through what she'd just told me. She may be surrounded by privilege and luxury, but it wasn't a life I wanted to lead. She stayed with Blaine because of the social status. There were no tears shed because she'd lost the man she planned to marry. Could Lila have lied about being in the bedroom at the time Blaine was pushed down the stairs? Maybe having Sabine at the party had been a step too far and Lila snapped.

Even I'd be tempted to shove Blaine down the stairs after everything he'd done to her.

And what was going on between James and Blaine? Why had they been arguing? I needed to have a chat with James and see where he was at the time of Blaine's murder. The suspect list was growing at an alarming rate.

I'd just gathered the coffee mugs and empty plates, when someone cleared their throat.

I looked up, and my breath caught. Campbell stood beside a bush, his hands clasped behind his back and his sunglasses on so I couldn't see the expression in his eyes. I doubted it would be a friendly one.

"A word please, Miss Holmes."

I gulped. I'd been caught snooping. I had a feeling I was about to be in a whole lot of trouble.

Chapter 9

"I'm busy," I said. "I need to get these things back to the kitchen."

Campbell strolled over and took the tray from my hands before setting it down on the table. "No, you don't."

I had to tackle this head on, before he sent me to the dungeon or whisked me away to a secret government compound never to be seen again. I bet Campbell could do either and get away with it. "Before you start complaining, I wasn't doing anything wrong. I spotted a woman in need of comfort. I couldn't ignore her in her hour of need."

"I'm sure that's all it was." One side of his mouth quirked up. "I hear you're into your fitness fads."

My eyebrows shot up. I wasn't expecting that. "I am."

"I've got a challenge for you. Are you willing to accept?"

"That all depends on what the challenge is."

"My teams need to be in the peak of physical fitness in order to do this job."

"Standing around outside doors and guarding people does take up a lot of energy."

He snorted a laugh. "It's more involved than that. We need to be ready at a moment's notice in case danger strikes."

"Okay, that's good to know, but what does this have to do with my challenge?"

"My teams do regular military style workouts."

"Oh, sure. I've seen you around the grounds. You get up even earlier than me to work out."

"We do. How about you try it out? Are you strong enough to complete a military challenge?"

I was intrigued. A military workout. I'd never done anything like that before. "Bring it on. When do you want to do it?"

"Have you had a lunch break yet?"

"No, I was just about to take it. Why, do you want to do it now?"

"It's best not to try this when you have a stomach full of food."

I grimaced. What was I getting myself into?

"Go and get changed," Campbell said. "I'll meet you around the side of the castle by the organic fruit orchard in ten minutes."

I couldn't help but smile. There I was, expecting a dressing down for poking around in Blaine's murder, and Campbell was offering to help me get in shape.

After returning the things to the kitchen and letting Chef Heston know I was on my break, I raced to my apartment, got changed into my workout gear, and jogged around the side of the castle.

My mouth fell open when I took in the scene in front of me. There were two giant tractor wheels, two long lengths of rope, and a row of smaller tires lined up. There was also a net that had been pinned just above the ground.

"This is what you use to work out? I thought you just went jogging?"

"We jog too. That's the warmup. How about we start with ten minutes of jogging to ease you in?" Campbell had also changed and wore a fitted khaki green top and rather shockingly short shorts that showed off his muscular legs.

My nose wrinkled, but I nodded. I wasn't the biggest fan of jogging. "Let's take it slow."

"Where's the fun in that? Come on, let's move."

I was gasping and had a stitch in my side after we'd completed our ten minutes of jogging. It was more sprinting than jogging, but Campbell was barely out of breath by the time we returned to the workout equipment he'd laid out.

"Woof, woof, woof, woof."

"It sounds like somebody wants to join us," Campbell said.

I was bent over at the waist, sucking in a few deep breaths and rubbing the stitch in my side. "He must have heard us out here. Do you mind if I let him loose?"

"Sure. He's so small, I won't even notice him."

I chuckled. "Don't be so certain about that. Meatball is small but mighty." I hurried away, grateful to have a few minutes of respite so I could get my breath back.

Meatball was out of his kennel, looking around. His ears pricked and his tail wagged wildly as he saw me.

"Hello, gorgeous boy. Do you want to see me make a fool of myself in front of Campbell? I have a feeling he's planning to work me to death."

"Woof woof!"

"Let's go then." I walked back around the side of the castle with Meatball.

He trotted over to Campbell and sniffed around his sneakers before wandering off to inspect the row of tires.

"Let's start with some strength training," Campbell said. "You're going to move that tractor tire from one side of the gravel to the other."

My eyes widened as I stared at the tire. "How do you expect me to move that? It's larger than me."

"Use your ingenuity. You're good at solving puzzles."

I walked slowly around the tire. It was enormous. Maybe I could get something to pry it off the ground and then flip it over. I looked around but didn't see any strong pieces of wood I could use as a lever.

"What are you waiting for? Has this mystery got you stumped?" Campbell said.

I slid him a sideways glance. He was enjoying himself. This must be his way of punishing me for interfering in the investigation. He may think he was clever, but I wasn't admitting defeat.

"Woof woof." Meatball bounced in and out of the smaller tires on the ground, clearly enjoying himself.

"Your dog's got the right idea," Campbell said. "Give it a go and see what you can manage."

I wrapped my fingers underneath the edge of the tire and tried to lift it. It didn't shift an inch.

"Bend fully at the knees, or you'll pull a muscle in your back."

I squatted and tried again. The tire moved. "I did it!"

"Now straighten it up and flip it over."

I dropped the tire back on the ground. "Are you kidding me?"

"No jokes, Holmes. Move that tire. I'll show you how it's done." He grabbed the other tire and flipped it like it weighed no more than a bag of sugar.

I gritted my teeth and dug in. I wasn't going to be beaten. If I couldn't flip this tire, Campbell would be smug about it for the rest of my days here.

I squatted as low as possible, got a good hold on the tire, and began to heave. I got it up a few inches, and my arm muscles protested.

"You've almost got it. Don't give up now."

I grunted as a trickle of sweat slid down the side of my face. The tire moved up a bit more. I just needed to get it upright and it would be easy to knock over.

"Do you need a hand?" Campbell asked.

"I've got it." A strange, strangled gurgling sound came out of my mouth. The tire slid, and I gasped, almost losing my grip. I dug my heels into the gravel and shoved all my weight behind the tire. It moved again. Suddenly, it was easier to lift. With one last mighty shove, I got the tire upright. I leaped in the air and whooped.

"Now get it over and do it again."

I turned to Campbell, my mouth open.

He chuckled. "Or are you ready to admit defeat?"

I almost was. Getting the tire upright had nearly killed me. I shoved and kicked it until it flipped over, sending up a cloud of dust as it slammed into the gravel.

I managed two more tire rotations before my stomach was heaving and my muscles trembled. I slumped over the tire as black dots appeared in my vision.

"Not bad. I have a couple of guys on my team who can only manage five rotations," Campbell said. He strode over and patted my shoulder. "It's amazing what stubbornness can make a person do."

I flopped over and lay on my back, staring up at him. "Is that it?"

"We're only just getting started. We've got the net crawl, the tire run, and then the rope slap."

I groaned and rolled onto my hands and knees.

A bottle of water appeared beside me.

I grabbed it from Campbell's hand and gulped most of it down.

He helped me to stand, an amused smile on his face. "Having fun yet?"

I lifted my chin. My lungs were burning and my legs wobbled. "Actually, I am. Bring on the next challenge."

The net crawl was good fun, especially when Meatball joined me.

I scrabbled along on my hands and knees under the low net. Meatball raced along beside me for a few seconds before barrelling under the net and squirming onto my back.

"Good work, Meatball," Campbell said. "The extra weight will make it more challenging for Holly."

Meatball licked the sweat off the back of my neck, more than happy to travel in style as I crawled under the net getting dusty.

Once I was out the other side, he bounced off and ran around me barking, as if telling me that he wanted another ride.

"Tire run next," Campbell said.

"Just give me a minute." I sucked in a few deep breaths. "Why aren't you joining in?"

"I can if you like. I've already done it once today."

"And you're still standing?"

"This is easy. You should try the extreme ultramarathon I take part in every year in Norway."

I grimaced. "What does that involve?"

"You jump off the back of a car ferry, swim the fjord, cycle one hundred and eighty kilometers, and then run a full marathon. The cycling is mainly uphill."

I felt queasy at the thought of all that extreme exercise. "That sounds like fun."

"It's epic. Tire run, now."

I headed over to the tires, and after a stumbling start, realized I needed to keep my knees high to avoid getting trapped in the next tire. I made it to the end in one piece.

"All done?" I asked.

"You've completed the first run. Now repeat it two more times."

I jogged back to the start and did it all over again.

"Just the ropes to do and you're finished," Campbell said.

"What do we do with the ropes?"

"Lift them up and down as fast as you can," he said. "They're tied to that tree."

I walked over to the two thick coils of rope. "What's this supposed to do?"

"It's great at strengthening your arms. It gives you a good cardio workout and helps to build muscle."

As soon as I started flipping the ropes up and down, Meatball raced over and grabbed one of them.

"Stop that! This isn't a giant chew toy."

Campbell looked on as I battled with Meatball, who clung on tight with his teeth as I tried to flip the rope.

"You're not helping. Let go of the rope."

"You stay right where you are, Meatball," Campbell said. "This will help Holly build her strength."

Meatball growled as he swung backward and forward as I flipped the rope, his tail wagging like it was on steroids.

"Keep going," Campbell said.

I managed another thirty seconds before collapsing in a sweaty heap on the ground. I was done in. My body felt like it had turned into a jelly. Everything wobbled, my lungs burned, and I felt woozy.

"Have some more water." Campbell handed me another bottle.

I drank it down before slowly standing to my feet. "How did I do?"

"Pretty decent. And after all that exercise, I'm hungry."

"How can you be hungry? You didn't do anything."

"Watching you has worked up an appetite. What have you got in the kitchen?"

"I've just fed most of the cake to Lila."

"I can only imagine what you were discussing while you ate that cake."

I swiped my hand across my brow. "I'm sure I can find you something. Meet me back at the bench." I staggered to the kitchen, grabbed my latest attempt at making the spice and vanilla jumbles, and headed back out.

Campbell was waiting by the bench I'd sat at with Lila.

I slumped into a seat before my legs gave out on me and placed the food down.

"What are these?" He lifted one of the jumbles and turned it over in his hand.

"Tudor desserts. It's a recipe I've been perfecting."

He took a bite as he sat. "It's got a weird texture."

"I tried a different type of flour in this one. It's a brand that has been traditionally milled. What do you think?"

Campbell ate several pieces of jumble. "Not bad. Not my favorite recipe of yours, though. So, what did Lila tell you about Blaine?"

"What makes you think we were talking about Blaine?"

"Don't treat me like an idiot, Holly. I knew you wouldn't be able to resist poking around in this murder."

"You're certain it was murder?"

"It was. And since you noticed the injuries on the body, you know that as well."

I lowered my piece of vanilla jumble. "How do you know about that? I only told Alice my suspicions."

"Don't forget, the castle walls have ears." He grinned at me.

"More like superspy bugs," I said.

"Something like that. What do you think of Lila as a suspect in Blaine's murder?"

"She has a great motive. Lila is the cheated-on girlfriend. She told me she was on her own when Blaine was found. She woke to find the bed empty and heard people shouting about what had happened."

"That's what she told my team," Campbell said. "Do you believe her?"

"Lila's definitely not your typical grieving girlfriend. She came across as a bit scheming."

"I agree. She was after the money and status Blaine offered her," Campbell said. "She'll be looking for her next target to latch onto. Lord Rupert needs to watch his back."

I choked on my piece of jumble. "She's not the kind of woman he likes."

Campbell smirked. "And you know that how?"

I grabbed another piece of jumble and ate it.

He grinned again. "Lila's a social climber but not necessarily a killer. She knew she was onto a good thing and was prepared to wait for Blaine to get worn down by her demands. She'd have gotten a ring on her finger, eventually."

"What a way to do it. Get the man of your dreams by always hanging around like a bad smell. I'll pass on that option when it comes to finding a man."

"Anyone else on your radar?"

"Sure. If this was a crime of passion, Sabine's the next obvious choice. The mistress has to be on the list. Maybe she got sick of waiting in the wings in the hope that Blaine would give up on Lila. He could have told her that was never going to happen, and she snapped. In a jealous rage, she shoved him down the stairs."

He nodded. "Sabine Novak. I've talked to her. She's definitely bitter, but similar to Lila, she knew she was onto a good thing. Apparently, Blaine was generous with his gifts. She didn't seem to mind being the kept woman."

"Okay. Then there's Percy and Lady Diana."

"You have them as suspects?"

"Lady Diana admitted she wasn't fond of Blaine. She was worried he was leading Percy astray. Although I did wonder if Lady Diana may have strayed with Blaine."

"Huh! That I didn't see. Did she confess that to you?"

"No, but Percy and Lady Diana were shifty and tense when we had breakfast together, as if they had something to hide."

"You had breakfast with Lady Diana?"

"I guess there must be some things your superspy bugs miss," I said.

He grunted. "Perhaps I need to speak to them again just to cover that base."

"I don't have them at the top of my suspect list. And Lila mentioned something odd when we were talking. She saw James Postle arguing with Blaine on the day of his death. She didn't know what it was about, but James wasn't happy."

"He's on the list to speak to, but I haven't got around to him yet."

"I spoke to him on the afternoon of the party. He seems like a decent guy. Friendly, laid-back. Nice."

"And not giving you the killer vibe?"

"I'm not always attuned to the killer vibe," I said. "But it wouldn't hurt to have a conversation with him."

"Anyone else?"

"That's everyone I can think of," I said.

He rubbed his hands together and stood. "Thanks for the food. But this stops now."

"What are you talking about? Me sneaking you treats from the kitchen?"

"Your investigation into Blaine's murder has come to an end."

"Why? I'm happy to help. We both identified the same suspects. I could be of use to you. People don't mind talking to me."

"Because you bribe them with your cakes."

"It's not bribery if someone wants to eat my cakes," I said. "And if having sweet treats softens a person up and gets them to reveal things they otherwise wouldn't, that's a good thing. You shouldn't shut me out of this."

"I'm not shutting you out. You weren't in in the first place. You're good at noticing things other people miss, but you're not that good. You've missed a suspect."

"Who have I missed?"

Campbell's eyes glittered. "That's on a need to know basis."

I glared at him. "Go on, Mr. Double-O-Superspy, why don't you share? Tell me who I've missed."

"Blaine had a public enemy. She openly declared that she'd kill him. She even posted her threats online."

"Who'd be stupid enough to do that?"

"Henrietta Audley."

Chapter 10

Campbell was already turning and walking away as I scrambled to my feet.

"Wait! What are you talking about? It can't be one of the Duchess's daughters."

He wheeled around and clamped a hand over my mouth. "This goes no further. You're to stop investigating this murder now. If Princess Henrietta was involved, we need to handle it carefully and with the utmost of discretion."

I pulled his hand away from my mouth and stepped back. "It can't be her. Why would she want Blaine dead?"

"You don't need to know that."

"I do. It's important. I mean—"

"It's not important to you. Stay out of this."

"Hold on a second, was that the only reason you were talking to me? You wanted to know if I'd worked out that Henrietta Audley could be the killer."

His eyes thinned to tiny slits. "Don't talk about this to anybody else."

Anger flooded my veins and my knees shook again, but not with exhaustion this time. "You weren't speaking to me about this investigation because you thought I could be helpful, you were using me."

"Wrong. I was extracting information to make sure the family name isn't sullied. I was simply doing my job."

This was outrageous. "I would never sully their name. I work for them. That would be a ridiculous thing to do."

"People do ridiculous things when there are large sums of money involved. The press would pay a lot to get their hands on a scandal like this. Even if it turns out not to be true, once Princess Henrietta's name is associated with this murder, it'll leave a stain."

My mouth opened and closed several times as I tried to get my thoughts coherent. "You think I'd do that? I'd sell a scandal to the press?"

Campbell shrugged. "Money makes people talk, much like your cake. You work in the kitchen at the castle, that's never going to make you rich."

I could barely breathe. How could he think I'd do such a thing? I loved my job, and sure, it didn't pay well, but I didn't do this to make endless amounts of cash. I did it because I got satisfaction from seeing people's eyes light up in pleasure when they tasted something I'd made.

"You … you …" I was too angry to form a proper sentence.

"This is your one and only warning, Holly. It's crucially important this situation is handled sensitively. Reputations are at stake."

"I know that now! And I would have handled it sensitively if I'd known a member of the family may be involved." I jammed my hands on my hips. "You don't trust me."

"I don't trust anybody. Don't take it personally."

Anger flared inside me again. I shoved Campbell in the chest. He didn't move.

I tried to kick him in the shin, but he simply dodged me. That only made my anger worse.

"I thought we were friends." I glared up at him.

"I don't have friends. And if you want to hurt me, you need to get in some training first."

As much as I wanted to punch him as hard as possible in the chest, I'd most likely break every bone in my hand.

"Thanks for the cake." He turned and walked away.

"Woof." Meatball nudged my calf with his nose.

"No, I am absolutely not fine. Campbell's the biggest jerk. He used me to get information, and he doesn't trust me." It hurt that he didn't consider me a friend. We had our moments of locking horns, but I thought he'd opened a door to me. He no longer saw me simply as an annoyance but someone he could trust. It had all been a charade.

"We'll show him, Meatball. I'll solve this murder. Campbell Milligan isn't going to use me and get away with it."

I was still rubbing the sleep out of my eyes the next morning as I hurried to the servants' staircase with Alice and Meatball. Wedged between us was a life-size crash test dummy.

"I can't believe you got this to arrive so quickly," I said.

Alice flashed me a grin. "Being a princess with a platinum card has its perks. It was a genius idea of yours to run these tests."

After my fight with Campbell yesterday, I was all the more determined to solve this mystery. A chat with Alice, the use of her platinum card, and we were in business.

I figured that if we threw a dummy roughly the size of Blaine down the stairs a few times, it should help us figure out how strong his attacker was and the force they'd used to kill him.

"This could be just what we need to get a break in this case," I said.

"And see whether the sneaky Sabine or the frustrated Lila had anything to do with it," Alice said.

I'd given her an update on the suspects in this murder while we'd ordered the dummy. Although I'd yet to mention that Henrietta could be involved. I still wasn't sure what I felt about that.

We arrived at the top of the stairs. I peered down them into the gloominess at the bottom. There was no window to provide any natural light, and it felt eerie.

"Are you looking for Blaine's ghost?" Alice giggled. "Granny hasn't seen him yet, but he may show up. I'll send him your way if he does, shall I?"

"You keep the castle ghosts far away from me," I said. "Let's start with a simple shove. Nothing too strong. Something you'd do if you were playing around with someone."

Alice balanced the dummy while I stood in front of it and pushed the chest. The dummy dropped down the stairs, hit the steps a third of the way down, and slid to the bottom.

Meatball yipped before racing down the steps. He grabbed the foot of the dummy and tried to drag it back up, growling as he did so.

"That definitely wasn't how Blaine was discovered," Alice said. "He was sort of sitting up with his back against the wall."

"Which means he was shoved harder. Someone would have needed muscle behind the shove."

"Or motivation," Alice said. "Although Blaine was drunk that night. Maybe the killer didn't need to shove that hard if Blaine was already unstable on his feet."

I hurried down the stairs and hauled the dummy back up, helped by Meatball, who was determined not to let go of the dummy's foot.

Once we were back at the top of the stairs, I picked up Meatball to stop him chewing on the dummy, and we repeated the exercise. This time, I shoved the dummy much harder.

It flew down the stairs, hit the mid-point of the stone steps, and slid to the bottom.

Meatball squirmed so much that I had to let him go. He charged off, his tail up as he jumped on top of the dummy and growled.

"That still didn't do it." Alice stood with her hands on her hips, staring down at the dummy. "Someone must have shoved Blaine hard to get him flying down the stairs."

"It would have been someone strong or someone raging mad," I said. "If this was the result of an accidental shove, Blaine should have been able to stop himself from falling, or wouldn't have landed at the bottom. He'd have hit the stairs and stopped."

"Let's have one more go," Alice said. "This time, we'll both shove the dummy as hard as we can. See if that gets it to the bottom of the stairs without hitting them on the way down."

I hurried down, extracted the dummy's fingers from Meatball's mouth, and pulled it back up the stairs.

Meatball bounced around and snapped at the dummy as if it was his worst enemy.

With Meatball tucked under one arm and safely out of the way, we balanced the dummy at the top of the stairs and both gave it a hearty push.

The dummy flew through the air and crashed at the bottom of the stairs.

There was a shriek, and something clattered to the ground. "What in the heavens is this?"

I grimaced at Alice before racing down the stairs. That sounded like Betsy Malone. I rounded the corner and saw her standing with her hands clasped against her chest, cleaning supplies scattered around her.

"Oh, Betsy! I'm so sorry. We didn't think anyone would be using the stairs this early in the morning."

"What are you doing with this thing?" Betsy peered at the dummy on the floor.

"Um, we're just doing some ... experiments."

"My heart nearly gave out on me when it almost landed on my head." Betsy blew out a breath.

"Let me help you with your things." I knelt and grabbed up her cleaning supplies.

"No, you won't put them in the right place. I have a specific order for my sprays, polishes, and oils. I know exactly where everything is. Don't make a muddle." Betsy grabbed up the tins of polish and began placing them in her cleaning caddy.

I handed them all to her, not sure how to explain what we were doing.

"So, are you going to tell me what this is all about?" Betsy straightened and glared at me.

Alice hurried down the stairs with Meatball beside her. "Good morning, Betsy."

"Princess Alice! You're involved with this too?" She arched an eyebrow at me. "Holly, I hope you're not leading young Alice astray."

"Of course, she isn't," Alice said. "We're doing a fun experiment. This is our corpse."

I shook my head at Alice, but it was too late. The crash test dummy was out of the bag.

"Corpse! Does this have something to do with the death of that young man?" Betsy's eyes widened, and she pursed her lips. "The whole village is alive with gossip. They know something's afoot in the castle."

"Um, maybe we shouldn't talk about it," I said.

"You absolutely should. I work here. I have a right to know what's going on." Betsy jutted her chin out. "Come on, tell me everything. Is this supposed to be the body of Blaine Masters?"

"It is," Alice said. "We're trying to figure out how hard he was shoved down the stairs to see who we can rule out as the killer."

"It's just a working theory," I said, silently willing Alice to stop talking.

"Shoved down the stairs? That confirms it then, definitely a murder." Betsy shook her head, her eyes gleaming. This new piece of gossip would be around the village in next to no time. "Have you figured out who killed him?"

"Not yet, but Holly is working it out," Alice said. "She's great at puzzles."

I sometimes wished I had an off switch when it came to Alice.

"We just wondered what happened to Blaine, that's all," I said. "How did you hear about his fall?"

"I was in the pub, and this beautiful young lady with long red hair came in. She was upset about something and was downing champagne like it was water. She was being comforted by a chubby ginger man. I've seen him at the castle before," Betsy said.

That sounded like Sabine and James. "Did you hear why she was so upset?"

"I heard snippets, but I don't like to listen into somebody's private conversation." Betsy pulled herself upright. "Anyway, they were talking about an accident at the castle. Of course, I had to listen in then. I was worried it might be something to do with a family member."

"What did they say?" I asked.

"That it wasn't an accident. The woman kept alternating between saying she was sad Blaine was dead and that he deserved it." Betsy looked sharply at the dummy. "You don't think that young lady in the pub had anything to do with it?"

"I'm sure the police will figure out what's going on," I said.

"More likely that you will." Betsy rubbed her hands together. "I can't wait to tell Pamela what's going on. We were talking about it just this morning on my way into the castle."

"You probably shouldn't tell anyone," I said. "This is an active investigation. We don't want any suspects getting wind of what's happening and making a run for it."

"Oh! Well, they won't hear anything from me," Betsy said. "I'm the soul of discretion. There's just a few people that have to know right away."

Betsy's gossip grapevine was more effective than the internet for spreading news. She had a group of friends who met in the pub once a week to discuss the latest rumors in Audley St. Mary. I had to shut this down before it got out of hand.

"I'm making fairy cakes today," I said. "Triple chocolate with a vanilla whipped cream. I know they're your favorite."

She patted her stomach. "I really shouldn't. I'm supposed to be on a diet before my holiday. Still, fairy cakes are small. I expect they have hardly any calories in them."

"That's right," I said. "I can make you a batch if you'd like."

Betsy stared down at the dummy again. "How about we call it a batch of twenty fairy cakes and a bottle of gin? Purely for medicinal purposes, you understand. If I have those, I'll be so busy enjoying myself that I'll forget what I saw this morning. How does that sound?"

"That sounds like a deal." I grinned at Alice. "Come by the kitchen when you've finished your shift. The fairy cakes will be waiting for you. And I'll get the gin delivered to your house later."

Betsy's mouth twisted to the side. It was most likely causing her physical pain to keep this new piece of gossip to herself. "Your fairy cakes are worth my silence. But the next time you go throwing life-size dummies down the stairs, make sure you see who's coming up them. That thing almost landed on me."

"Sorry again, Betsy," I said.

Alice hugged her. "We'd never want to hurt you, Betsy. You're the best cleaner in the whole castle."

"That's enough of that." Betsy stepped back, her cheeks flushed. "I'm only doing my job. Now, get this dummy out of the way so I can get on with my work. There are plenty of rooms that need cleaning." She grabbed her cleaning caddy and hurried up the stairs, muttering to herself.

"That was close," Alice said. "Good move with the bribery. I wouldn't have thought of that. I was thinking that we'd have to take Betsy to the dungeon to ensure her silence."

"My way is less deadly, and I'm sure Betsy will appreciate it. I trust her to stay quiet for now," I said.

"And this wasn't a waste of time," Alice said. "We now know that whoever shoved Blaine did it deliberately. They'd have needed to run at him to get enough power to knock him down the stairs so he landed the way he did."

I collected the dummy and slid a glance at Alice. "Would you say your cousin, Henrietta, is strong?"

"Henrietta! Not really. She's not an avid exerciser like you are. Why do you ask?"

"You haven't heard?" I couldn't put it off any longer. Alice needed to know that the finger of suspicion was pointed at a member of her family.

"Holly, what aren't you telling me?" She grabbed my arm. "What's Blaine's murder got to do with Henrietta?"

"Campbell has her on his suspect list. She's got a hate campaign running that's focused on Blaine."

"Oh my goodness. Of course! I'd forgotten about that. It's her blog that showcases men with more money than sense. It's actually quite funny." Alice's eyes widened. "But wait, Campbell can't seriously think that Henrietta was involved with this?"

"He does. He's been looking into what she's posted online. Apparently, she threatened to kill Blaine."

"That's nothing. That's just her way. Henrietta thinks words are more powerful than anything else. And she's worse than Rupert when it comes to reading. Instead of bringing a case load of clothes with her to this party, she brought a trunk of books. She's impossible. She spends her life daydreaming about fictional worlds."

"Did you know about the posts she's got online about Blaine?" I asked.

"Sure. She doesn't keep them a secret."

"Why does she hate Blaine so much?"

"I'll let Henrietta tell you that." Alice scooped an arm around the dummy and took some of the weight. "We have to speak to her. And you need to make sure Campbell no longer believes she's a suspect in this murder."

Chapter 11

After concealing the dummy in Alice's bedroom, we raced to Henrietta's room. I checked my watch. It was still early; Henrietta was probably asleep.

Alice rounded the corner in front of me. She stopped so fast that I bashed into her.

"What's the matter?" I asked.

She backed away and turned to me. "There's a guard outside Henrietta's bedroom."

"That must be Campbell's doing," I said. "He must be worried Henrietta might make a run for it."

"We have to get in and see her," Alice said. "When you get to know her, you'll realize she couldn't possibly be a killer. Although I suppose if someone tried to steal her favorite book she might club them over the head with it. That wasn't how Blaine was killed, so we don't need to worry about that."

"I'll be on the lookout for any dangerous book shaped weapons lying around when I get in there." I peered around the corner. "How do you suggest we do that with a guard blocking our way?"

"You leave that to me." She fluffed up her blonde hair and pouted. "I'm sure the charming guard outside the door won't be able to ignore my pleas for help. What man can resist a damsel in distress?"

"What are you going to say you need help with?"

She chewed on her bottom lip for a few seconds. "I could tell him I'm lost."

"You live in this castle."

"It's a big place. There are a lot of rooms that all look the same." She peeped around the corner. "I've got it. I heard a strange noise in my bedroom. I'm worried there's an intruder in the castle."

"That might bring a whole security team to investigate. We want no guards, not a small army to deal with."

"How about I saw a stranger in the grounds? I could say I was worried about my safety. I'll insist the guard investigates."

"That could work. All I need is ten minutes with Henrietta," I said.

"Let's try that." Alice pulled out her phone. "I'll message Henrietta so she knows you're not some ax murderer creeping in to lop her head off."

"Good thinking. I don't want any book related injuries when I surprise her with an early morning wake up call."

Alice grinned as she tucked her phone away. "Wish me luck." She turned and hurried along the corridor toward the guard.

I peeked around the corner with Meatball. Alice approached the guard and pointed out the windows. I could just detect the frantic tone of her voice.

Within a few seconds, she'd dragged the guard away, along the corridor and out of sight.

Once they were gone, I made my move. I dashed along the corridor with Meatball and snuck open Henrietta's bedroom door.

The curtains were shut, so it was gloomy inside the room, but I could make out someone lying on the bed. I hurried to a window and pulled open the curtains.

"I don't want to be disturbed," a sleepy voice came from the bed.

"I'm really sorry to interrupt your sleep, Princess Henrietta," I said. "Alice sent me."

"Alice? What's she up to?"

"She knows you're in trouble. She wants to help."

Henrietta sat bolt upright. Her light brown hair was pulled off her face, and she wore pink pajamas with unicorns on. "Who are you? How do you know Alice?"

"I'm Holly Holmes. We're friends," I said. "She thinks I may be able to help you. Check your phone. She sent a message, so you'd know I was genuine."

Her gaze drifted to Meatball as she lifted her phone from the nightstand. "Is that one of Mommy's corgis?"

"No, he's mine."

Meatball wagged his tail as he sniffed around the room.

"Who are you again? I'm never good first thing in the morning. Especially not when I'm awoken by a stranger."

"I'm a friend. I'm not here to cause any trouble," I said.

Henrietta grabbed a glass of water from the nightstand and took a sip as she read the message on her phone. "Holly's the best. She'll stop you going down for murder. Much love, Alice."

I grimaced. That wasn't the perfect message for Alice to send, but it got the salient points across.

Henrietta's gaze ran over me. "Did you go to school with Alice?"

"No, I work in the kitchen. We don't have much time. Did you know, there's a guard posted outside your door?"

She set her glass back down and frowned. "I did. That idiot security man told me he didn't want me leaving the castle. I said I'd do exactly what I wanted. He couldn't tell me what to do. That's when he informed me less than politely that there would be a guard monitoring my movements. He made me feel like a prisoner. I complained to Mommy, and she said she'd have a word with him, but she also told me off."

"What did she tell you off about?"

Henrietta was silent for several seconds. "Alice trusts you?"

"She does. And I trust her."

"Very well. My so-called smear campaign was the issue Mommy wasn't happy about," Henrietta said.

"The campaign against Blaine?"

She lifted a hand before dropping it back on the bed. "That man was a monster. He lived for the sheer pleasure of hurting other people. He had the morals of an alley cat, and anyone who stood up to him was sure to be ruined."

"Is that what you did? You questioned him, so he got back at you?"

Henrietta's gaze slid to the side. "I understand that I'm the plain one out of the sisters. The others all got the blonde locks and the bright blue eyes. They sometimes tease me and say I'm the runt of the litter."

"The runt of the litter!" I said. "Henrietta, you're beautiful."

"Don't worry about that. I know my own worth. It has nothing to do with how symmetrical my features are," she said, "but sometimes, even I feel a bit overwhelmed standing with my beautiful, perfect sisters. I'm not complaining. I have a good life, and I'm happy with it." Her hand rested briefly on the pile of books on her bedside table.

"You like to read," I said.

"I do. I study too. I got my PhD from Cambridge four years ago. I studied medieval poetry and the classics. Did you go to university?"

"Yes, I studied history."

"And now you're surrounded by it. A good career choice. I value learning and education above everything else. I'm not necessarily talking about books, but taking the time to think about your place in the world is important. As is making sure you know the value of giving back and helping others."

I nodded. "I imagine that when you encountered Blaine and his materialistic life, you didn't approve."

She pulled her long hair over one shoulder. "Blaine was an example of everything that's wrong with society. He had to have the latest model of car or the most expensive pair of shoes. He had no care for the costs those things had on the environment. Think of all the money that could be donated to a charity, rather than wasting it on an extravagant car. Of course, if I'd suggested that to Blaine, he'd have thought I was ridiculous."

"But that's what you did?"

She sighed. "Not quite. I was forced to go to a party. We all have to attend them, do the social circuit, the usual upper class nonsense. I grudgingly attended and had the misfortune to bump into Blaine. He had girls fawning around him, and he was drunk. He tried to quote Shakespeare to look impressive. He got it completely wrong, so I corrected him."

"I can imagine how well he took that," I said.

"He called me plain and a shrew. Blaine said the only reason I was at the party was because of my family name. He said I was invisible to men, and that I'd only ever find somebody because I was rich. I stood up for myself, but then the women around him set about me too. Soon, he had half the room laughing along with him and his spiteful comments. I had enough. I was a coward, and I ran away." Princess Henrietta gathered her knees up to her chin. "I should have stamped on his foot and thrown a drink in his face, but sometimes, when you're surrounded by beautiful people all the time, it gets to you. Men don't value intelligence and stimulating conversation. They want long blonde hair and women who flatter them. I'm never going to do that. Certainly not to a man like Blaine."

"After that, you decided to get back at Blaine?"

"The world needed to know what a feckless individual he was. I started up an online blog. Every time he wasted money, got drunk, or made an exhibition of himself, I blogged about it. And when I could get my hands on them, I'd post pictures as well. Do you know, in the last year, he wasted over two million pounds buying wine? Wine! That could have been sent to orphanages abroad, invested in conservation projects, or gone into saving the public libraries. And that was just the tip of the iceberg."

I glanced at the closed door. As interesting as this was, I didn't have much time. "Campbell thinks you wanted to kill Blaine. Did you put anything like that on your blog?"

"I ... well, it's no secret. Anyone can read it. Why don't you take a look?" She lifted her phone from the bedside table, opened a webpage, and handed it to me.

I scrolled through the information, my eyes widening as I read. "You suggested drowning Blaine in a vat of the wine he bought."

"I've also suggested running him over with one of his ridiculously expensive cars." Henrietta shrugged. "Maybe not my proudest moments. But he made me so angry at that party."

I handed her back the phone. "That was a horrible thing for him to do to you. It was wrong."

"That was Blaine. So long as he was having fun, he didn't care who got hurt or humiliated."

"Has Campbell questioned you about what happened to Blaine?"

She tucked her phone back on the bedside cabinet. "He has. He keeps focusing on my blog and the comments I made. As I keep telling him, only an idiot would publicly post that they want to kill somebody and then do it. It's such an obvious evidence trail. I hated Blaine and I didn't hide that fact, but I didn't do anything to him at the anniversary party."

"Do you mind telling me where you were when Blaine was killed?"

"I can, but it won't help me out of this mess. I wasn't in my room. I find parties hyper-stimulating and have trouble sleeping after I've been to one. Rather than toss and turn most of the night, I went for a walk in the grounds. I was on my own. No one can vouch for me." She shrugged. "It's a terrible alibi. I've been over it in my head several times to find ways to substantiate my whereabouts, but I was alone. It's how I spend most of my time. I don't enjoy the company of other people on the whole. Besides, no one else would have been awake that late to come with me. I know the castle grounds well, having grown up here as a child. I decided a walk might tire me enough so I could sleep."

"And where were you when Blaine was discovered?"

"I was just about to come in the front door of the castle," she said. "Lights flicked on, which surprised me. Then I heard shouting and went to see what was going on. I didn't stick around when I heard Blaine had been in an accident. I wanted nothing to do with him. I went to my room and sat up reading. My sister, Diana, came in to tell me what was going on. I promise you, I didn't do this."

Princess Henrietta had a very clear motive and a terrible alibi. I could understand why Campbell was looking hard at her for this murder, but she was also right. If you were planning to kill somebody, you wouldn't post about it online.

"If you had to point the finger at anybody for what happened to Blaine, who would it be?" I asked.

"That's easy. His personal assistant, Sabine Novak. She's been hanging around Blaine for months. She goes to all his business events and parties. She made it clear that she wanted Blaine all to herself."

"Have you spoken to her about their relationship?"

"Only once. I'd sometimes go to parties Blaine attended, to get soundbites for my blog. I'd go in disguise so nobody recognized me. One night, I was at the bar when Sabine staggered over. She was angry about Blaine and made an offhand comment about how lucky he was to have her. Then she pulled out a credit card he'd given her, she told me that as well, and ordered a bottle of champagne. I could see exactly why she wanted him. Money smooths over a lot of relationship cracks."

"I haven't spoken to Sabine," I said, "but I did see her arguing with his real girlfriend, Lila."

"They're as bad as each other," Henrietta said. "They were both in it for the money and the social status. They used him just like he used them. But Sabine was on a different level of obsession. In her twisted mind, I think she actually loved him. She even set up a Blaine fan page online."

"She did what?"

"I know, very much not normal. Here, take a look." Henrietta scrolled through her phone before handing it to me.

There was a webpage devoted to Blaine Masters. It was full of pictures of him, usually wearing a suit or tuxedo with a drink in his hand and a smug smile on his face.

"How do you know this page is run by Sabine?" I asked.

"Any idiot can upload photos," Henrietta said. "It was easy for me to learn where the webpage originated from. That's her handiwork. In Sabine's weird world, she thought she could have a happily ever after with Blaine."

I jumped as someone knocked on the bedroom door.

Henrietta cocked her head. "Hold on a moment, how did you get in here if there's a guard outside?"

"That's an interesting story," I said. "Do you mind if I hide somewhere? I'm probably not supposed to be talking to you."

The knock came again. "It's your cleaning service, Princess Henrietta."

A breath whooshed out of me. That was Betsy's voice. "She's fine. You can let her in."

"Sure. Come in," Henrietta said, a curious look on her face.

Betsy hurried in backward, pulling in a cleaning cart, and closed the door behind her. She turned and stared at me. "What in the heavens are you doing in here? The last I saw of you, you were throwing that ..." She glanced at Henrietta. "That thing on the staircase."

"This is linked to that thing on the staircase," I said.

"What thing are we talking about?" Henrietta asked.

How was I going to explain this? Princess Henrietta would think something was wrong with me if she found out about the crash test dummy experiments.

"Did you know there's a guard outside the door?" Betsy asked. "I had to argue to get in here to change the towels and make sure the bathroom was spotless for the princess."

"The guard's back?" I glanced at the door. Alice was supposed to keep him away. Something must have gone wrong.

"I bet he won't think much of you sneaking around in here," Betsy said. "And why are you in here?"

"Um, well, that's a good question. How strong are you, Betsy?" I looked at the trolley she'd pulled into the room.

"Probably fitter than you, my girl. All this cleaning gives me muscles. Why do you ask?"

"Could you squeeze Meatball and me in your cleaning cart and still push it?"

"Well I never!" She stared at me as if I'd taken leave of my senses.

"Betsy, I need your help," I said. "If I get discovered in here and Campbell learns about it, I'll be in trouble. He's already told me to keep my nose out of this investigation."

Betsy chuckled and shook her head. "And of course, you're not going to listen to the head of security for Audley Castle. Why would you do such a sensible thing?"

It was time to lay my cards on the table. I had to get out of here. "Princess Henrietta was helping me with some questions I had about Blaine's murder. She knew him when he was alive."

Betsy's mouth opened and closed several times. "Oh, well, that does sound important."

"And Princess Alice insisted I help. I can hardly go against the command of a princess," I said.

"Hmm, I suppose not." Betsy turned and rooted through her cleaning cart.

"I'm at your mercy. Please, you're my only hope." I pressed my hands together in a prayer position.

"Stop begging. I'll help. If I unload most of my towels and the dirty sheets, you'll be able to fit. You'll have to squeeze in a bit though. And you need to keep that dog quiet. If he makes so much as a squeak, we'll be discovered."

"Meatball will be on his best behavior," I said. "He doesn't want to get caught either."

Meatball cocked his head and whined.

"Give me five minutes in the bathroom, and we'll get you settled." Betsy hurried into the attached bathroom.

I glanced at Princess Henrietta and saw a smirk on her face. "I've had a few run-ins with the head of security. He thinks I'm nosy."

Her smirk morphed into a smile. "You absolutely are. But I like that about you. And if you help to clear my name, I'm grateful for it. I'm also grateful to Alice for getting you involved."

"She knows you're innocent," I said. "She only wants to help."

"Oh, I know that. Alice is sweet. She's one of the good ones. People underestimate her."

"I never do," I said.

"Good thing too. I'm glad you're friends with Alice. She hasn't had the easiest of times in this family. Have you ever met her parents?"

"No, they've not visited the castle since I started working here."

"Let's just say, they follow social etiquette to the letter. With Alice's two failed engagements behind her, they as good as abandoned her here. Fortunately, my parents welcomed Alice with open arms. Still, it's not nice to have your parents give up on you because you don't choose a so-called suitable man to be seen with. Better to be single than to settle."

Alice rarely talked about her failed engagements, or her parents, other than to complain about them. "She'll always have a friend in me."

"Come on, Holly. Let's sneak you and Meatball out of here before I change my mind about helping you." Betsy returned from the bathroom and swiftly unloaded everything.

I peered into the empty cart. It would be tight, but I reckoned we'd fit.

I hopped over the edge of the cart and stepped into it. I ducked down, almost folding myself in half to fit.

"Get your head down another inch," Betsy said. "I can cover you with a few towels. And if I balance my cleaning supplies on top, it won't look odd."

I heard Meatball whine. "Grab Meatball for me. He's worrying that he'll be left behind."

Betsy grumbled as she lowered Meatball in, and after some careful shuffling around, I got him wedged beneath my knees.

"Be a good boy now. No noise."

He licked my hand, his tail wagging. This was an adventure for him.

"We're ready to be covered," I said.

Betsy placed several large white fluffy towels on top of my head. "If I get caught doing this, I'm not taking the blame."

"You can say I forced you into it," I said. "I bribed you with fairy cakes and gin."

"I'll be doubling my order of those," Betsy said. "And I quite fancy an economy sized bottle of that pink flavored gin they've been selling down the pub."

"You'll get it all, I promise. So long as I get out of here."

"Good luck, Holly," Henrietta said.

I lifted a hand and raised a thumb before sliding back into the cart.

Betsy pushed the cart a few inches. "Goodness! I can tell you enjoy your own cupcakes."

"It's important to taste test," I muttered.

"Right. Heave ho. I can do this."

I heard Betsy open the door. I kept a tight hold on Meatball as the cart was slowly pushed into the hallway.

"All done," Betsy said. "Towels changed. Bathroom spotless."

"Move along then," the guard said.

One of the cart's wheels squeaked as she pushed it along the corridor.

I held my breath until I felt the cart turn a corner.

The towels were removed from my head, and Betsy peered down at me. "All clear."

I handed her Meatball before hopping out. "Thanks for that, Betsy."

"You be careful, Holly. Don't go getting yourself in trouble. You don't want to lose your job. Who will supply me with fairy cakes if you're not here?"

"I will be careful, but I don't want someone innocent charged with Blaine's murder," I said.

Her eyes widened, and her hand flew to her mouth. "Of course! That's why the guard was there. You don't think … you think Princess Henrietta—"

"No! Don't even go there. I'm just covering all the bases."

"I wish I hadn't made that deal with you over the fairy cakes and the gin. Pamela would fall off her seat in shock if she heard that Princess Henrietta Audley could be involved with this terrible business."

"Betsy, I'm begging you, don't let a word of this get out. I'll give you fairy cakes for the rest of the year if you keep quiet. It's so important this doesn't get spread around the village."

She sucked in a deep breath. "I've worked for this family for over twenty years. I'm a gossip about the small things that go on, but I'd never muddy up someone's name. Princess Henrietta is always kind to me. That's when her nose isn't buried in a book. Of course, this is just between us."

I gave her a brief hug. "Thanks, Betsy." I looked along the corridor. "Did you see Princess Alice on your travels?"

"No, I haven't seen her. Now, I must get on. I'm behind on my duties because of you."

I thanked her one last time before walking around the castle, trying to find Alice, but there was no sign of her.

I scooped up Meatball and cuddled him. As much as I wanted to discount Princess Henrietta in this investigation, I couldn't just yet.

I needed to clear her name, and to do that I had to find the real killer.

And I knew just where to go next. Sabine Novak's name had been mentioned too many times, and with the weird webpage postings about Blaine, I had to assume she was an obsessive, jealous lover.

But just how jealous had she been?

Chapter 12

"Holly, go to the store and pull together these items." Chef Heston handed me a long list of baking ingredients.

"On it, Chef." I finished stacking the caramel and pecan tray bakes in the fridge before washing my hands and heading outside. It had been a busy day in the café. Four coachloads of tourists had arrived a few hours ago and were munching their way through the entire display case of sandwiches, cakes, and ice cream in the café.

I'd barely had time to think about Blaine's murder and the suspects since this morning.

I'd just opened the store beside the kitchen, when a car door slammed.

I walked back a few steps and peered around the side of the castle. A brilliant white Lamborghini was parked outside the main entrance.

A moment later, Sabine stepped out of the castle and took a large pair of sunglasses out of her purse.

It looked like she was leaving, and I hadn't talked to her about what went down between her and Blaine. She couldn't go before I'd done that.

Two of the Duchess's corgis romped out of the entrance behind Sabine.

"Shoo! Get away from me! Scram." She waved her hands at the dogs and sidestepped them so fast that she lost her balance on her high heels and stumbled to the ground.

The corgis yipped around her before racing back into the castle.

"Wretched things!" She threw her purse at the retreating corgis.

I hurried over and helped her up. "Are you okay?"

"Of course I'm not. The Duchess's dogs are out of control. One almost bit me at breakfast. Disgusting creatures. I can't understand why anyone would want an animal you have to pick up after."

"I'm guessing that you're more of a cat person?"

"Fetch my purse." Sabine brushed my hand away from her arm. "I'm not an any animal person. What's the point of keeping something that sheds fur, demands you feed it, then you have to clean up after it? It's almost as bad as having a baby."

I grabbed the purse and returned it to her. Now I had the chance to question Sabine, I wasn't letting it slide by, despite her rudeness. "I recognize you from the anniversary party. You knew Blaine Masters, didn't you?"

"If you must know, I was his personal assistant." She straightened her red pencil skirt and smoothed her hands over the fabric.

"I'm sorry for your loss. You must have been close if you worked together every day."

"What's it to you?"

"Oh! Nothing really."

She peered over the top of her sunglasses at me. "And who exactly are you?"

"Holly. A friend of the family."

Sabine removed her sunglasses. "You know the Audleys?"

"I'm good friends with Princess Alice," I said.

"Lucky you." Sabine looked around. "Where's my driver?"

"You're leaving?"

"Unfortunately not. That jumped up gorilla in a suit has given me permission to go out for the afternoon so long as I'm supervised. As if I need supervision to have my hair cut. The way he spoke to me made me feel like a criminal. This whole situation is a joke."

"It's scary what happened to Blaine. Everyone's talking about it."

"No doubt they are."

"Have you been questioned?"

She slid a glare my way. "Why the interest in Blaine? Don't tell me you're another one of his women. You're a little on the chunky side for him."

I wasn't chunky. I was a healthy weight and had plenty of muscle. "What if I was involved with Blaine? That wouldn't be a problem for you, would it?"

She stepped closer, and her nostrils flared. "You want me to believe that you dated Blaine Masters? Are you sure we're talking about the same man?"

"We definitely are. Tall, good-looking, rich. He arrived here in a red sports car with his actual girlfriend, Lila."

She smirked. "Lila was barely his girlfriend. Although she liked to tell everyone she was. The woman's deluded. As, I suspect, are you. Blaine wouldn't have been interested in you."

"But he was interested in you?"

She looked away as her foot tapped on the ground. "Where is that driver? I swear, if he keeps me waiting any longer, he'll be out of work."

"Blaine was a ladies' man," I said. "That didn't bother you?"

She sighed. "I had nothing to worry about. We had an understanding."

"You were more than his personal assistant?"

"And if I was? Don't get jealous on me. I've handled enough of his flings to know you won't be a problem."

"I'm definitely not jealous."

Sabine shrugged. "Not that I care if you are. I was Blaine's personal assistant in every sense of the word. And I've never heard of you, so you weren't important to him. What was it, a drunken one-night fling? You got him drunk and seduced him, thinking you could be seen with him and make a name for yourself."

I shuddered at the repulsive idea. "Something like that." Sabine's jealousy was making her talk, so I'd keep on prodding.

"You wouldn't have been worth remembering," Sabine said.

"I know I was nothing to Blaine, but he must have liked you a lot since he gave you a job. Was he serious about you?"

"Of course he was serious about me. Blaine loved me. He was leaving Lila after they'd been on their Caribbean holiday. It was all paid for, so he didn't want to cause a fuss by breaking up with her until they got back. That would have made things awkward."

How charitable of him. "You were happy for him to go away on holiday with Lila?"

"Blaine arranged for me to have a private suite at the hotel they were staying in. We'd have had plenty of time together. Lila would have been none the wiser. She's not what you'd call brains of Britain."

Wow! Blaine was a piece of work. He'd planned to take his girlfriend and his mistress on holiday. And he'd been lying to them, stringing them both along.

"Did you find it difficult, seeing Blaine with another woman?"

"I was happy to bide my time. Blaine was worth it. After the holiday, we were going to become exclusive."

"Lila didn't suspect a thing about your relationship?" I asked.

"I'm sure she had her doubts. Blaine wasn't known for his discretion when it came to women."

"Have you heard that the police are investigating Blaine's death as a murder?"

There was a pause, her face turned away from me. "I have."

"Is it possible that Lila did discover your relationship and decided to get her revenge?"

Sabine turned toward me. "She killed Blaine?"

"She would have been angry if she'd found out the truth," I said.

A pink rash of color flushed up Sabine's cheeks, poking through the thick layer of makeup she wore. "If that's true, I'll kill her. He was my meal ticket … I mean, he was my perfect guy. We had everything planned. I'd worked it out for us. He wouldn't leave Lila until after the holiday, so I booked the suite to make sure I'd be near him if he needed me. Now you're telling me that … that sneaky witch has taken him away from me."

"You must be heartbroken," I said.

"Lila's head will get broken if this is true." Sabine curled her fingers around my arm. "Did she tell you that she killed him?"

I tried to step away, but she clung on like a limpet. "No! But she may have overheard Blaine discussing your plans and put the pieces together."

She scowled before looking away and replacing her sunglasses. "When are the police arresting her?"

"I'm not sure they will. They're still talking to people from the party about what happened," I said. "That must be why the castle security team needs you to stay here."

She shrugged. "It's no hardship staying in Audley Castle with people waiting on me hand and foot. I'll speak to the police and tell them everything I know about Lila if it makes them arrest her. I kept telling Blaine he should just get on with it, make us official, and get rid of her. Lila was old news. She was getting wrinkles, despite having Botox."

"Have you been asked where you were at the time of Blaine's death?"

"Of course. I was taking a shower. I'd been in there about five minutes when there was a knock on my door. It was a security guard checking I was safe. I rushed out to see what was going on and discovered Blaine at the bottom of the stairs. It was horrible."

I thought back to that night. I had seen Sabine at the crime scene. She'd been wearing a dressing gown and was standing with James, but her hair had been dry. She hadn't been in the shower. She was lying about her alibi.

"Other than Lila, can you think of anyone who might have wanted to harm Blaine?" My mind played with Sabine's alibi as I continued to question her. Had anyone else noticed that her hair hadn't been wet that night? Had she just given herself away as the killer?

"Have you had the misfortune to meet Henrietta Audley? Better known as The Shrew?" Sabine said.

"I have."

"She needs looking into. She's unstable. Henrietta attacked Blaine at every opportunity. She was always smearing his name online. Of course, no one takes her seriously. She has no friends and next to no social life. The police need to keep an eye on her. Personally, I think it's all a front."

"A front for what?"

"The Shrew is desperately in love with Blaine and violently jealous of anybody who was involved with him.

She wanted him to herself. And because he teased her a bit one evening, she turned nasty. If Lila didn't kill Blaine, Henrietta must have been involved."

Footsteps approached, and the door behind us was pulled open. A member of Campbell's security team stepped out.

"I've been waiting five minutes," Sabine said. "You'll make me late for my hair appointment."

"My apologies, miss." He opened the door to the car. "I'll make sure you're not late."

"I'll report you if we are." Sabine stepped into the car.

I stood and watched her being driven away. Something didn't feel right. Sabine lied about what she was doing when Blaine's body had been discovered. And in the panic after he'd been found, it was unlikely anyone else would have noticed that her hair wasn't wet from being in the shower.

Maybe she'd decided she'd had enough. Blaine was lying to her, no doubt cheating on her with numerous women, and the hassle of being with him could have been more trouble than it was worth. What if she'd arranged to meet him that night, knowing he'd had too much to drink? She could have waited at the top of the servants' stairs and shoved him down.

Sabine had a good motive and a poor alibi, plus she'd just lied to me. I needed to talk this through with someone.

I turned and slammed into a solid wall of muscle. I staggered back and stared up.

Campbell was standing right behind me.

Chapter 13

"Don't sneak up on me like that!" I took a few steps away from Campbell. How much of my conversation with Sabine had he heard?

"What are you doing?" he asked.

"Going back to the kitchen. I need to collect items from the storeroom." I turned to walk away, but Campbell grabbed hold of my arm.

"You were talking to a suspect in this murder investigation."

I pulled my arm out of his grip. I still hadn't forgiven him for manipulating me. "What if I was?"

"I doubt you were sharing fashion tips."

"Maybe we were. I have excellent fashion sense. I happen to wear my work uniform extremely well."

One side of his mouth tipped up. "What do you think of Sabine?"

"She's an entitled money grubber who'd look a lot sexier if she gained a stone in weight. The bony look isn't healthy."

A smile slid across his face. "At least we agree on something. Talking of putting on weight, I hear there are chocolate dipped horns with vanilla whipped cream in the kitchen."

"And if there are? They're for paying customers, not the staff."

"I'm so much more than staff," Campbell said. "Grab a couple and we can talk."

"We're talking now? I thought you didn't want me involved."

"I'm having a moment of weakness. Take advantage of it. It won't last."

As tempted as I was to tell him to stick the cream horn where the sun didn't shine, I was fascinated by this mystery. There were so many people who wanted Blaine dead.

He tapped the side of my head. "Less thinking and more action."

"You'll have to help me in the store," I said. "I was out here getting supplies for Chef Heston when I saw Sabine. He'll be wondering where I am."

"I can haul bags of flour if I need to. Lead the way."

We spent the next ten minutes loading up a trolley in the kitchen store before I wheeled it back in and unloaded everything on the counter. "Chef, I'm taking my break now."

He waved a hand at me, his attention on the glazed apricot tarts in front of him.

I snuck two chocolate cream horns from the chiller cabinet and dashed outside. Campbell was already settled on the bench, so I joined him.

"What have you found out about—"

"Not yet. I need a fix of energy before I get interrogated by you." Campbell took a large bite of the cream horn. "This is good."

"Of course it is," I said. "What about Sabine?"

"You think she's good for the murder?"

"I think a lot of people are good for the murder," I said. "That's the problem. Don't you still have your sights set on Princess Henrietta?"

"She's not off the hook just yet," Campbell said. "My team have investigated her blog posts. She makes no bones about hating Blaine."

"And she has a poor alibi," I said.

"You know that how?"

"My insider sources," I said. "Princess Henrietta strikes me as an intelligent woman. Not the sort of obsessed fan who'd post about killing Blaine and then act on it."

"Sabine also has a fascinating internet history. That interests me much more."

"I've seen the webpage full of pictures of Blaine."

"It's so much more than that," Campbell said. "Have you heard of the Revenge Ex website?"

"I can't say I have. What's it about?"

"It has a twisted brilliance to it," Campbell said. "You can order all sorts of disgusting things to send to an ex. Most recently, Sabine arranged to have a weekly delivery of horse manure dumped on Blaine's doorstep at his London apartment."

I almost choked on my cream horn. "They're together. Why would she do that? Unless he ended the relationship. Maybe he was getting serious with Lila, and Sabine wouldn't accept it."

"That's just the start. She's also sent him glitter bombs and a cake made from ghost peppers."

I shook my head. "That's the hottest chili pepper going. Even a small amount will burn your tongue."

"There were also the garlic mints and the underwear containing itching powder. The list goes on."

"How long has Sabine been sending Blaine these things?"

"Three months," Campbell said.

"Which is weird. I mean, she's been working for him for six months. We have to assume the relationship was either going on before he employed her or it started soon after. Why would she do that to him?"

"I've never understood how a woman's mind works," Campbell said.

"All your superspy training hasn't helped you figure out the fairer sex?" I grinned at him. "I'm disappointed."

"Don't be. I excel in every other area."

I chewed on a piece of sweet pastry. Campbell was never short of ego. "That's why you're talking to me? You want to get a woman's view of this murder."

"Something like that."

"You need more women on your team."

"I already have three."

"Get more. We're excellent."

"I don't disagree."

I leaned back and closed my eyes. "I'm trying to think like Sabine. Maybe she was doing this to set somebody else up. She could have ordered those things in the hope Blaine would think they were coming from somebody else. Like his angry girlfriend who he was so obviously cheating on with half of London. Sabine could have been planting seeds of doubt in Blaine's mind about Lila. She told me they were going to become official after he'd been on holiday with Lila."

"The workings of the female mind are truly terrifying, but it could fit. Blaine saw Sabine as a bit of fun, but she wanted more. She tried to make Lila look crazy so she could step into her high heels when Blaine got rid of her."

"Sabine had an intense vibe about her when we spoke," I said. "I tried the sympathy card when I saw her waiting by that car, but she was dismissive. Then I alluded to the possibility that I'd been involved with Blaine."

"I bet that got her attention."

"It did. Sabine got mean. She also said that she'd kill Lila if she discovered she'd shoved Blaine down the stairs. Sabine wasn't in the relationship for love."

"From the way Sabine went through Blaine's money, that was obvious," Campbell said. "We ran her credit history. He gave her a personal credit card. She spent up to the maximum limit every month. Fifty grand gone on restaurants, clothes, and weekends away."

I whistled. "Maybe Blaine got tired of her excesses and cut her off."

"No, her card was still active when we checked the records. He could have told her to put the brakes on the spending, though."

"Which led to an argument, and she shoved him down the stairs," I said. "I don't know, though. Sabine said that Blaine was her meal ticket. Would she kill such a generous meal ticket?"

"What about the crazy gifts she'd been sending him? That's not the workings of a rational mind. Maybe she was sending him those things because she'd begun to loathe him."

"That's possible. Sabine wanted his money and the lifestyle, but she also wanted to get revenge for his cheating ways. We've all done things we aren't proud of when a relationship is in trouble. I bet you've done your fair share of drunk dialing to your ex-girlfriends," I said.

Campbell grunted and stuffed the rest of the cream horn in his mouth.

"I take that as a yes. What did you do, turn up at three AM with music blaring and declaring your undying love? Go on, you can tell me."

"No, I can't. Moving on, I assume you asked about Sabine's whereabouts when Blaine's body was discovered."

I leaned forward. "I did. She lied to me."

"How do you know that?"

"Sabine told me she was in the shower."

"That's what she told my team. You think otherwise?"

"I do. Her hair wasn't wet when I saw her. She was wearing a dressing gown, but if you're in the shower you usually end up with wet hair. Even if you tie it up and put a cap on your head, those annoying tendril bits at the back of your neck always get damp. She wasn't in the shower when Blaine was killed."

His gaze narrowed. "And when were you going to mention this important piece of information to me?"

"Jeez, I just found out Sabine's alibi. I could have been coming to tell you about it."

"I doubt that. This is useful. It adds to the evidence we have against her. We have proof she was sending those weird gifts to Blaine, no one saw her at the time of his murder, she has a strong motive given she was the secret mistress or possibly the spurned mistress if Blaine called time on the affair. Add to that the fact she lied about her alibi. We're bringing her in for questioning."

I gestured at the road leading out of the castle. "You've just let her be driven away."

"With one of my top guys as her driver," Campbell said. "If she makes a run for it, he'll bring her down. We wanted to give her the illusion of freedom. And it worked. She slipped up and made a mistake with you. Now she's going to pay for it."

"You really think it was Sabine?"

"That's what we need to find out," Campbell said. "My money's now on her. That's where our focus will be." He stood and swiped up my half eaten cream horn.

"Hey! I was going to finish that."

"I've saved you the trouble." He ate it in two bites. "And a word of advice, the next time you want to play throw the crash test dummy down the stairs, let me know. I could have saved you the effort of buying a new one. We have a stash of them in storage." Campbell turned and walked away.

I stared after him and shook my head. Was there anything Campbell didn't know?

Chapter 14

I was up just after dawn the next day, a bundle of excited nerves swirling around my stomach. I had the morning off work and planned to make the most of it. My bag was packed full of towels, my swimming costume, and snacks. I'd given Meatball a quick run and a big breakfast before settling him in his kennel with a rawhide chew. That would keep him occupied for hours, and he wouldn't miss me while I went on my adventure.

I was catching the first bus into Cambridge to go to my very first mermaid class.

I'd read all about it online, and it sounded like a whole heap of fun. You got to be a mermaid, complete with fitted tail. You basically had to teach yourself a new swimming technique to stay afloat. I couldn't wait to get my mermaid tail on and enjoy a morning of swimming.

A loud thud had me glancing around. Rupert and James were striding across the front lawn, carrying bows and arrows. They must be doing archery practice. I'd seen Rupert several times honing his archery skills at the private practice ground they had in the woods.

I'd have been tempted to join in if I didn't have my mermaid class to get to. And I was determined not to miss it. I checked the time. I only had ten minutes to get to the bus stop, so had to get a move on.

I hadn't made it a dozen steps when something zipped over my head. I stopped and looked around. A few feet from me, an arrow was embedded in the grass.

"What the—" I dropped to the ground as another arrow flew past my nose. I was under attack!

Laughter rang out from behind a bush. A few seconds later, Alice appeared, a large bow in her hands and a quiver of arrows strapped across her back. "I almost got you."

"Are you crazy?" I scrambled to my feet and stared at the arrows. "You were trying to hit me?"

She waved the bow in the air. "Of course not. I'm an ace shot. I never miss. That was just a bit of fun to get your attention."

My mouth fell open. "Fun! That was too close."

"Stop being a stress-head. I won all the under eighteen archery tournaments at school. It's one of the few things I'm really good at. It's just a shame no one uses a bow and arrow anymore. I should have been part of Robin Hood's merry men. I'd fit right in. Where are you going?" She looked at my bag.

I rested a hand over my racing heart. "To the nearest emergency room. You almost gave me a heart attack."

"You're being silly. Come on, where are you sneaking off to?"

"I'm not sneaking anywhere," I said. "It's my morning off, so I'm going into Cambridge."

"Not going shopping by the looks of it."

I hesitated. "No, I'm going to mermaid school."

Alice inhaled sharply, and her eyes widened. "How exciting."

"I'm looking forward to it," I said. "I need to go, though. I'm catching the bus. If I miss that, I'll have to wait half an hour for the next one."

"Rupert, James! Get over here right now," Alice yelled. "We're going to mermaid school with Holly."

"Oh! Wait, no. I mean, you have to book in advance." I loved Alice, but sometimes I just wanted to do things on my own.

"I'm sure if we pay a bit extra they won't mind squeezing us in. Tell me everything about mermaid school."

"Um, well, it's a popular class. I'm sure there won't be room for you. And it's more the sort of thing women do. Rupert and James might not enjoy it."

"Holly! Don't be sexist. Men can be mermaids too. Or are they mermen?"

"Probably merman. I'm not sure they do the mermaid tails in a big enough size. They may have to order them in."

"Oh! Amazing! We get to have tails as well." Alice placed a hand against her forehead. "I've died and gone to heaven. We have to come. I insist upon it. And just think, it'll be a hoot to see Rupert and James in tails."

"What's all this?" Rupert strolled over with James. "Hello, Holly. You're up early."

I backed away a couple of steps. "I was just saying to Alice that I need to go. I've got a class this morning."

"And we're all going as well," Alice said. "It's mermaid school. Doesn't that sound fun? Rupert, call for a car. Holly said she's going on the bus. We can't have that."

Rupert rubbed the back of his neck. "I mean, of course, Holly is always welcome to use a car. Are you sure you want us to come with you?"

I shot him a grateful look. "I had planned on doing this on my own."

"It'll be so much more fun together," Alice said. "James, you'll come, won't you?"

James grinned at me. "Of course. I'm always happy to try something new. I'm not sure I have the right physique to be a mermaid, though." He flexed a chunky bicep.

"It'll be hilarious," Alice said. "Get the car, Rupert. We can't be late."

Rupert pulled out his phone and made a call to the house.

"And arrange to have our swimming things put in the trunk. James, you can borrow a pair of Rupert's swim shorts. Don't you wear those terribly small pants, Rupert? Will James fit in them?" Alice said.

Rupert glanced at me, and a blush spread up his cheeks. "They're more comfortable than those loose shorts people usually wear. I'm sure I've got something James can borrow."

Alice shook her head. "No matter. We'll be wearing our giant tails most of the time, anyway. I'm so glad I shot at you, Holly. This will be a great morning."

I guessed it would be fun with Alice and the guys tagging along. I shouldn't begrudge them the experience of being a mermaid. I'd been looking forward to it for weeks. "Sure, why not?"

"And then afterward, we can go and have lunch at my favorite restaurant in Cambridge."

Alice chatted on, and as she talked, James kept giving me discreet glances and smiling. Was he trying to get my attention?

Rupert appeared to have noticed too, and stepped in front of me, blocking James's view. He moved me away a few steps as he leaned close. "I hope you don't mind Alice inviting us all. She's always so enthusiastic about everything. She loves spending time with you. She's always telling me you're her best friend."

A warm glow filled my chest. It was selfish of me to do this on my own and not want them to come along. "Of course not. The more the merrier."

"I'll be honest, I'm not much of a swimmer. I suspect I'll sink when I have a tail on."

"I'm an excellent swimmer." James stepped around Rupert and clapped him on the shoulder. "I can give you a few pointers so you don't make a fool of yourself."

"I'm sure I can manage." Rupert frowned at James.

"Here's the car," Alice said. "Everybody put your archery gear in the trunk and hop in. Let's go to mermaid school."

James and Rupert jostled to be the first to open the back door of the car.

Alice giggled from behind her hand and she nudged me. "You've got admirers, Holly." She slid into a seat, and I followed her and settled my holdall on the floor of the car.

Was she serious about Rupert and James being keen on me? I'd been friendly to James when we'd met, but I barely knew the guy.

I gave the driver directions to the swim school in Cambridge, and we settled in our seats as the car slid along the driveway and onto the main road for the twenty-minute journey.

"I won several swimming competitions at school," James said. "We had to learn all kinds of survival techniques."

"I remember having to dive to the bottom of the swimming pool to pick up a brick in my pajamas," Alice said. "I could never figure out why we had to do it. You don't swim in your pajamas."

"Tell us more about mermaid school, Holly," James said. "I have no clue how a mermaid is supposed to swim. Is it difficult?"

"Using a mermaid tail should help you perfect a new swimming technique," I said. "You're forced to keep your legs together so you have to flip up and down just like a mermaid and power forward using your arms and tail."

"I wonder if we get to choose the color of our tails," Alice said. "I want a pink one. Although maybe blue would be better. Any color will be fine. I can't wait to get in the water."

"Do you like to swim, Holly?" James asked.

"I do," I said.

"Holly likes all kinds of fitness trends," Alice said. "We did goat yoga recently."

"And Holly loves goats," Rupert said.

I glanced from Rupert to James. "That's right. I do like goats."

"We'll have to go to the goat sanctuary again," Rupert said. "I'll adopt you some more goats."

"We did have a nice day there," I said. "But I'm already the proud adoptee of three adorable goats. I don't need any more."

"I'll take you to a zoo and adopt you an orangutan," James said. "We could even do a private tour. They do that for VIP guests. Once the zoo is closed, they take you on an evening trip and you get to see the animals without anyone else in the way. The keepers tell you all about them. I've even been in an enclosure and hand fed lemurs. They're funny creatures. Not the brightest of animals."

"We can do that too, Holly," Rupert said. "I know a chap who runs a lion sanctuary. I'll take you there."

"You can't have Holly hand feeding lions. She may not live to tell the tale," James said. "Stick with me and my lemurs."

Alice nudged me again and grinned.

I was desperately in need of a change of subject. "Have you spoken to Henrietta since I saw her?" I asked Alice.

"Oh, I have. She said you escaped in a linen cart. Is that true?"

"Yes. The guard came back before I was ready to leave," I said.

"That's all my fault. I tried to convince him to keep looking for the mysterious intruder, but he was having none of it. I was worried that you might have been caught."

"Thanks to Betsy, I got out."

"What's all this?" James asked.

"Holly is helping to solve Blaine's murder," Alice said.

"Henrietta can't be involved in this business with Blaine," Rupert said. "She's eccentric but has a kind heart."

"You're only fond of her because she loves books as much as you do," Alice said. "Actually, Henrietta would be perfect for you, James. She's clever, pretty when she makes the effort, which she rarely does, and she's as rich as they come. She's got her own estate up in Scotland."

James cleared his throat before patting his chest. "I've met Princess Henrietta several times. I'm not sure she's the right girl for me. I imagine she's charming, but I may have my eye on someone else."

"Holly's already taken if you're interested in her," Alice said.

James stared at me. "She is? I mean, you are?"

I pinched the bridge of my nose. Alice really wasn't helping. "My work keeps me busy. I don't have time for a relationship."

"Everyone has time for a relationship." Alice giggled. "I have a brilliant idea. James should marry Henrietta, then Rupert can marry Holly. You could have a joint wedding ceremony. I'll be bridesmaid to you both."

I wanted the ground to open up and swallow me.

"Steady on," Rupert said. "Who's talking about marriage?"

"Quite right," James said. "I mean, Holly, you're a charming lady. I'm sure any man you marry will feel privileged to be in your life. But … but …"

I lifted a hand. "I'm not marrying anyone. Alice is only teasing." I stood less than gently on her foot in the hope it would shut her up.

"Never?" Rupert asked. "Don't you want to get married one day?"

I stifled a groan and shot a glare at Alice. This was all her fault. "Honestly, I don't think about it much. Getting back to Henrietta, you're certain she's innocent?"

"She absolutely is," Alice said. "She went walking that evening, which is typical of her. She's always been a loner."

"Do you know what happened between her and Blaine to make her hate him so much? She told me a little and showed me her blog."

"Oh, that. I felt so sorry for Henrietta after it happened. She was forced to go to this fancy party. Everyone was going to be there, all the important names. She tried to get out of it as she does with all events, but she was forced into it. So, she made an effort, she had her hair done nicely and got a new dress. Henrietta looked lovely that night. It all went wrong when she said something to Blaine. He humiliated her in front of everyone."

"She mentioned that to me."

"Blaine had all of his friends laughing at Henrietta. She was devastated. She disappeared from the party and basically disappeared from society life for several months. Henrietta pretends she's independent and nothing bothers her, but she has a fragile ego. It was blasted apart by Blaine and his meanness. I even heard she went into therapy to deal with it."

"She doesn't sound like the most stable of girls," James said. "I'm not sure I'd be happy to marry someone like that."

"Oh, she's absolutely crazy, but in a good way," Alice said. "Henrietta's no killer. She didn't kill Blaine."

"I'm glad you're confident about Henrietta's innocence," I said. "I like her."

"I'd bet my head under the guillotine that she isn't involved," Alice said. "If I'm wrong, you have permission to chop off my head."

"Let's hope it doesn't come to that," James said.

"It won't," Alice said.

"I agree," I said. "With Sabine now in the spotlight, Campbell believes the case is closed. He just needs her to make a confession."

"I'm glad to hear that," James said. "I'd hate to think of a murderer prowling around and putting you lovely ladies at risk."

"Us lovely ladies can take care of ourselves," Alice said. "But it's nice to have a knight in shining armor as a backup."

James grinned before turning to Rupert. "Have you caught any of the cricket this season?"

Alice leaned closer to me. "Are you certain it was Sabine?"

I tilted my head from side to side. "Eighty percent sure. Although there are lots of good motives for wanting Blaine dead. A jealous, out of control secret mistress has to be top of the suspect list."

"And all the other suspects must have been questioned by now," Alice said.

I glanced at James. He was deep in conversation with Rupert. "James's name was mentioned by another suspect. He was seen arguing with Blaine before the party."

Alice's eyes widened. Before I could stop her, she tapped James on the knee. "We have a question for you."

I grimaced, not knowing where to look. I should have kept my mouth shut.

"What's the question?" James asked.

"Did you kill Blaine Masters?"

James drew back in his seat and clutched the edge. "What makes you ask that? Of course I didn't kill him."

"Someone saw you arguing with him," Alice said. "What was all that about?"

James spluttered out several words before taking a deep breath. "I ... well, it was nothing. I saw him scratch my car. He parked too close and slammed his door into mine. He didn't even stop to see if he'd caused any damage. I went to take a look and discovered a scratch and a dent. I charged after Blaine and confronted him about it."

"How did he take that?" I asked.

James glanced at me. "He was amused. He said my car needed to be taken to the junkyard. That's a Triumph Herald 1200. There are less than a thousand still on the road. All he did was smirk and tell me to send in the bill. He wished me luck in getting him to pay it. I saw red, but I'd never kill a chap over a scratched car."

"Campbell has verified all of this?" I asked.

James rubbed a hand down his face. "Of course. And my alibi is Caroline Audley. I was talking to her when Blaine was discovered."

"Oh, yes! That's right. I remember now," Alice said. "You were one of the late hangers on at the party." She glanced at me. "Caroline is terrible. She'll party until dawn if she gets the chance."

"I'm much the same," James said. "We grabbed a bottle of the sparkling stuff and kept on partying in the games room. Caroline will confirm it."

"She already has," Alice said. "I mean, I didn't ask her where you were when Blaine was killed, but she told me you were up until the early hours together."

It was a pity she hadn't remembered that before she started this cringe inducing conversation.

"That's right. I had nothing to do with what happened to Blaine," James said. "I hope you believe me."

"We do," Alice said. "That's such a relief. You can cross another name off your suspect list, Holly."

I repressed a groan as I forced a smile. Maybe I wouldn't survive mermaid school. At this rate, it would be a blessed relief.

Chapter 15

"Pay attention to these important rules before we begin today's session," Dita Brey, our instructor for the morning, said. "You must be able to swim at least twenty-five meters without help and without stopping."

"Tick. I can do that," Alice said.

"You must also be able to tread water and be able to do a full rotation."

"Tick again." Alice grinned at me.

"Float on your back in a star position and flip onto your front without any help," Dita said.

"Easy peasy," Alice said.

"And don't mind putting your head under the water," Dita said. "All mermaids must be able to glide effortlessly while being fully submersed."

"I'm not a fan of that idea," Rupert said. "The chlorine always stings my eyes."

"That doesn't bother me," James said. "I could swim the length of this pool with my eyes open."

"I'll do it if I have to," Rupert said.

"You must also be comfortable using breast stroke and your new tail at the same time. And remember, a happy mermaid is a safe mermaid. Any questions, just ask." Dita smiled as she looked around the group of twenty apprentice mermaids. "Now, everybody practice flipping their tails backward and forward and get used to the movement."

Once we'd arrived at the swimming pool, Alice had sweet-talked herself, Rupert, and James into the class with a little gentle bribery and a lot of eyelash fluttering. We'd been given multi-colored mermaid tails and joined the rest of the class just before it began. We had the exclusive use of the main pool for the next two hours, so we could mermaid to our hearts' content.

"This is harder than it looks." James panted, his face bright red as he flailed his tail around.

"It'll be easier once we're in the water," I said.

Alice flipped her tail like an expert. "I was born to be a mermaid. I can't wait to get going."

"If everyone is comfortable in their tails, I want you to divide into pairs and get in the pool. Remember, you now have your mermaid fins so you won't be able to stand. You'll damage your tail if you stand on it. Use your arms to keep yourself upright in the water, and when you feel confident, lift your tail up and try that same movement you're doing now," Dita said.

"I'll pair up with you," James and Rupert said at the same time.

"One of you has to come with me," Alice said. "Come on, James. You can be my partner."

"Oh, well, if you're sure." He glanced at me.

"Of course, I'm sure. Just make sure you don't let me drown," Alice said.

"Everyone shuffle to the edge of the pool and prepare to enter the water for your first time as a mermaid," Dita said. "Try not to scrape your tails as you get in. Think of them as a living extension to your own body. Tails have feelings too."

"You look good as a mermaid," Rupert said to me. "I'm not sure I'm made for a tail." He adjusted the too tight blue and pink tail that was pulled over his swimming trunks.

"You're doing great," I said.

The class had been brilliant so far. Dita had been teaching people how to be mermaids for five years. She'd been patient with all of us as we'd struggled to get into our tails. And now, it was time to enter the water. It was the moment I'd been waiting for.

I gasped as I entered the pool and my tail tried to flip me upside down. It was only Rupert's steadying hand that kept me from going under.

"Thanks," I said as I struggled to get my balance.

"Maybe humans simply aren't meant to have tails," Rupert said.

"Don't be a spoilsport." Alice flipped around in the water effortlessly. "Having a tail is such fun."

I watched her with no small degree of envy as she mastered her tail with ease. I was determined to become good at being a mermaid.

"With your partner's help, practice floating on the surface of the water while keeping your tail up," Dita said. "You need to adjust to a new sense of balance with your extra load."

"Where shall I position my hands?" Rupert's cheeks were bright red. "I don't want to be ... inappropriate."

"I'd never call you that," I said, charmed by the fact he'd asked before grabbing hold of me. "Try under my stomach and arms." I stretched my arms out in front of me and tried to get my balance right. I flipped my tail up, over correcting, and ended up upside down in the water.

Rupert caught hold of me and spun me around.

I spluttered as I emerged and blinked teardrops of pool water out of my eyes.

"Try gentle movements to begin with," Dita said from the side of the pool.

I tried again, and Rupert caught me as I flipped my tail up. I balanced on his arms as I got a feel for my tail and spent a few minutes adjusting my balance as I flipped, twisted, and turned.

"You're doing great," Rupert said.

I grinned at him. This was fun.

"That's excellent, everyone. Now swap around and give your partner a chance to practice," Dita said.

Thanks to the water's buoyancy, it was no struggle to keep Rupert afloat with his large tail.

He bobbed on the surface for several seconds. "I'm getting the hang of this." He flipped his tail backward and forward.

"We'll make a merman out of you yet," I said.

"Now that everyone's got a feel for their tail, I want you to practice forward motion," Dita said. "Remember, you won't be able to kick your legs, so make full use of your tail fins and either front crawl with your arms or breaststroke. When you're confident with that move, we can try some underwater swimming with your arms by your sides."

"I'm more of a doggy paddle kind of guy," Rupert whispered.

I laughed as I bobbed in the water.

The next ten minutes were a blur of splashing, gasping, and almost drowning. I just about managed to keep afloat for five seconds while doing the breaststroke, and slightly longer doing a front crawl.

I pushed my tail down and swam my hands through the water to keep afloat as I looked around to see how everyone else was doing. Alice was on the other side of the pool, laughing as she dove and spun. James didn't look quite as comfortable as he clung to the side, his face bright red.

I did a full turn in the water. There was no sign of Rupert.

I looked around the group, wondering if he was helping somebody else and had gotten distracted, but he was nowhere to be seen.

My eyes widened as a hand shot out from the surface of the pool. That looked like Rupert's blond hair under the water. I took a deep breath and dove under, grabbing hold of the hand just as it lowered, and yanked Rupert above the surface.

He shot upright, spitting water everywhere.

"What happened?" I clutched the tops of his arms, my heart racing.

"Thanks, Holly! I got tangled in my tail." He sucked in air as he coughed and spluttered some more.

I kept my hands under his armpits to make sure he stayed afloat as he caught his breath. "You gave me a fright when I couldn't see you."

He pushed his hair off his face. "I was doing fine. Swimming along quite merrily, then it felt like my tail got twisted. I peeked under the water to take a look and overbalanced. Next thing, I was spinning. I'm definitely not meant to have a tail. I'm a dry land person."

"Everyone gets better with practice," I said. "I'm just glad you're okay."

His gaze met mine, and he smiled. "Today hasn't been so bad. I got to spend time with you."

I realized how close we were and let go of Rupert, causing him to duck back under the water. "Oh! Sorry." I pulled him out again.

He rubbed his eyes. "I might take a break. You go have fun with the others." He doggy paddled to the edge of the pool.

I sighed. I wasn't developing feelings for him. Rupert wasn't for me, and neither was the lifestyle he led. I'd simply saved a friend in trouble.

"I'm so glad I caught you this morning, Holly," Alice said, her damp hair tied off her face as we sat in the back of the limo on our way back to the castle. "I'd never have thought of taking part in mermaid school."

"You're a natural mermaid," I said.

"I am, aren't I? I couldn't believe it. The second I put that tail on, it felt like it had been made for me. I'll have to get some tails for all of us. We can go swimming in the lake in the grounds."

James and Rupert exchanged a glance.

"My merman effort was a one-off," James said. "I couldn't stay afloat long enough to get any motion."

"I was much the same," Rupert said. "And getting tangled in my own tail made me a bit nervous to keep swimming. You got really good though, Holly."

"I enjoyed myself," I said. "I'd like to do it again."

"It's settled," Alice said. "I'll hire someone to make our mermaid tails. My treat, a way of saying thank you for letting us butt in on your morning off."

I sat back in my seat, tired, smelling mildly of chlorine, but happy. I was glad they'd come with me. It had been a lot of fun.

Once I was back at the castle, I hurried to my apartment. I got changed into my work uniform and headed over to Meatball's kennel.

He greeted me as if he hadn't seen me in months, launching himself out of the kennel, literally jumping into my arms, before licking my face.

I laughed as I cuddled him before setting him back on the ground. "Did you have a good morning?"

"Woof woof." He wagged his tail.

"I got to be a mermaid," I said. "It's a lot harder than it looks. My legs will ache for days."

"Woof woof." He sounded like he knew exactly what I was talking about.

"Let's give you a quick run around and some food, then I need to get to work."

Meatball happily obliged, and after a ten-minute trot around so he could do his business, he was settled back in his kennel with more food.

I'd only just stepped into the kitchen when Chef Heston strode over and slapped a piece of paper down on the table. "We need to talk."

"I'm not late, am I?" I glanced at the clock. I was right on time.

"It's not about your timekeeping, which can be dubious at best. What's this?" He jabbed a finger at the piece of paper.

I peered at it. "I don't know. It looks like a reference request."

"With your name on it," Chef Heston said. "You're planning on leaving?"

I grabbed up the paper and read it thoroughly. It did have my name on it. "No! I haven't applied for another job. This must be a mistake. Who sent you this?"

"Lorcan Blaze."

I dropped the piece of paper, feeling a little dizzy. "That's impossible. He hates me. He didn't even like my food."

"You must have made an impression on him when you went to see him the other day. He wants you on his team."

"Oh, that. I didn't think he was being serious," I said.

Chef Heston's eyes narrowed. "He has spoken to you about this? He's made you an offer?"

"Not a genuine one. Lorcan was just showing off. He claimed that members of his team got to travel the world and do anything they wanted with their careers after being trained by him."

"That's not showing off, that's the truth," Chef Heston said. "When people do well under him, they go on to bigger and better things. Did you tell him you were interested in this job?"

"No! I like my job here."

He shrugged and grabbed up the reference. "It doesn't bother me either way. You're replaceable."

My mouth dropped open. "I am? Don't you love the desserts I make for the castle café?"

"Anyone can make a good dessert. I'll fill this in and send it back to Lorcan, shall I?"

I blinked, not knowing what to say. I hadn't asked Lorcan for a job. Sure, for a second, I'd felt flattered that he'd wanted me on his team, but I had no plans to leave the castle.

"Get on with your work, Holly," Chef Heston said.

I watched him walk away, still too stunned to speak. Chef Heston didn't value me as a member of his team. I was replaceable. My gut clenched as anger trickled through me. Maybe I should take up Lorcan's job offer. If I was that easy to replace, there was no harm in trying something new. And it was complicated here. I always had Campbell breathing down my neck every time I put a foot wrong, and then there was the trouble with Rupert. He was a lovely guy, and I was fond of him, but nothing could ever happen between us. And now this. My boss just told me I wasn't valued.

I looked around the kitchen, my heart feeling bruised as I saw the people I considered my friends hard at work.

Could I leave this behind? I could always reinvent myself, open up another café. And this time, it would be a success. I'd make sure of it.

With a heavy heart and my feet dragging, I pulled out the ingredients to make a giant stack of vanilla whip cupcakes. This situation needed serious thought and baking always helped to clear my head.

It could be time to move on, find a place where I was valued and respected. Maybe a change could be as good as a rest.

It was just past eight o'clock in the evening, and I was finally leaving the kitchen. My eyes were heavy and my stomach growled. I was more than ready for an early night, a cuddle with Meatball, and a huge dinner. Swimming always made me starving.

As I collected Meatball from his kennel, I mulled over what dinner to make. I had a lasagna in the freezer, or I could do a simple stir fry.

I slowed when I spotted Campbell leading Sabine out to a police car. He had a smug smile on his face as he placed her in the back of the car before thumping the top and standing back as he watched the car drive away.

It looked like the mystery of Blaine's murder had been solved.

I turned and trudged to my apartment. For some reason, it felt like a hollow victory. Maybe it was simply sour grapes because I hadn't beaten Campbell in figuring it out this time.

At least it was over. The murderer had been caught, and everything could get back to normal at the castle.

Meatball barked and raced ahead to the apartment door, sniffing around a small white cooler box left on my step.

"What have we here?" I bent and picked up the card sticking out of the side. I flipped it open and read it.

A reminder of the fun we had at the Giddy Goat sanctuary. With fondest regards, Rupert.

I sighed as I opened the lid of the cooler. Inside, were several chunks of goat's cheese, some oat crackers, grapes, and a jar of chutney.

At least now I knew what I'd have as a starter for dinner. I collected up the cooler, opened the door, and let Meatball in before walking in behind him.

I set the cooler down on the kitchen table and closed my eyes.

First thing tomorrow, I needed to make changes around here. I had to simplify my life. Simple was always better.

Chapter 16

The following day passed in a rush of cake baking, brownie testing, and being yelled at by Chef Heston, who seemed to be in a worse mood than usual.

I was glad when my shift finished. I grabbed the biggest vanilla whip cupcake from the chiller cabinet, put Meatball's leash on, and we headed into the grounds for a long walk. It would be good to have some time alone, clear my thoughts, and think about what I was going to do next.

I'd had a restless night of sleep as I'd mulled over everything that had happened yesterday. I was still in shock over Lorcan Blaze's bold move to get a reference about me. I should have been angry with him, but I was intrigued. Everything would change if I left the castle. I'd be leaving behind my friendship with Alice, and whatever relationship I had with Rupert. I wouldn't miss the long bike rides so much, panting and puffing up and down the hills of Audley St. Mary. But I would miss the village, the tightknit community, and the friends I'd made in my time here.

I unclipped Meatball's leash and let him run free. I took a large bite of the delicious vanilla whip cupcake and let the sweet taste carry away my worries for a short while. I didn't need to over-complicate things. And that's exactly what was happening here. I'd investigate my options. There was no harm in that.

Meatball barked as a strange bird called from up high in the distance. That didn't sound like any bird I'd heard before, but we got all kinds of rare birds in the woods.

The sound came again, drifting in the wind. Could it be a peacock?

"Woof woof!" Meatball's tail shot up and he raced away.

"No, you don't." I chased after him. "No bothering the local wildlife. That bird won't want to be friends with you." I jogged after him, stuffing down the rest of the cake as I did so.

The bird sounded like it was close to the castle, and that was the direction Meatball was heading.

It came again, louder this time. It was way above my head.

I peered up at the east turret, expecting to see a bird perched on the top, and spotted a hand waving out the window. That must be Lady Philippa.

Once I'd zeroed in on the sound, I realized it wasn't a bird at all. Lady Philippa was making that noise.

Meatball barked as he bounced up and down at the base of the east turret.

I caught hold of him and attached his leash. "That's enough. It looks like we're being summoned. Shall we go and see Lady Philippa? She may have a prediction about our future."

"Woof woof." He bounced up and down again, seeming thrilled with the idea of going up the east turret staircase. He always knew that when we got there, he'd be given treats.

"I imagine Lady Philippa won't want us to arrive empty-handed." I hurried back to the kitchen, tied Meatball up outside, and dashed in for more vanilla whip cupcakes.

I went back, collected Meatball, and we went around the side of the castle to the entrance that took us to the stone steps of the turret.

I took off Meatball's leash, and he scampered ahead, always eager to get up the stairs quickly to avoid the cold spots and strange whispers that often accompanied us.

I froze as a draft skimmed across the back of my neck. Someone was whispering behind me.

"Take heed," a quiet voice said.

I jerked my head around and looked down the stairs. There was no one there. There never was when I heard these weird disembodied voices.

I made it up another dozen stairs before something blew in my ear. I squeaked, and went up the stairs two at a time, until I'd reached the top.

Meatball was waiting for me by the closed door to Lady Philippa's apartment. He scratched a paw against it and whined.

"Maybe she hasn't heard you." I hurried over and joined him. I knocked on the door. "Lady Philippa, it's Holly and Meatball. We've brought you cake."

"Come in, the door's open," she said.

I tried the handle. It wouldn't budge. I twisted it several times, but it felt like it was locked. "Have you turned the key on your side? We can't get in."

"It's definitely open," Lady Philippa said. "Give it a shove with your shoulder."

I twisted the handle again and leaned my weight against the door. This door wasn't moving.

"If you're busy, we can always come back," I said.

"Oh! I see the problem. Get out of here, you pesky thing. Holly's a friend."

Meatball cocked his head, and I stared at the door. Who was she talking to?

A few seconds later, the door was pulled open. Lady Philippa stood there with a smile on her face. "At last! I thought I was going to die of hunger." She was dressed in a floor-length sapphire gown with an enormous green feather boa wrapped around her neck and trailing down her chest. She also had on a giant teased curly blonde wig.

"That's quite a look," I said.

She lifted her hands and twirled in a circle. "I'm channeling my inner Marilyn Monroe."

I glanced around her apartment. "Was someone blocking the door?"

"Yes, but take no notice of him. He always does that to get my attention. It was the blue man. He floats around being grumpy and trying to bring everyone's mood down. Come in." She took the plate of cupcakes from my hand and gestured us into the room.

I glanced around, a fair amount of nerves bubbling in my stomach as I looked for the blue man.

"Don't dawdle," Lady Philippa said. "He's gone now. And even if you do see him, he doesn't cause any trouble. Take a seat."

I'd just settled in a plush velvet seat opposite Lady Philippa, when there was a grumbling bark from the bedroom. Horatio, her ancient, bad-tempered corgi, waddled out. He took one look at Meatball and began to bark.

Meatball joined in, but when Horatio lumbered toward him, he bounced in the air and landed on my lap.

"Enough of that," Lady Philippa said. "It's rude to bark at our guests."

Horatio grumbled and circled the chair I sat in, his gaze on Meatball.

Lady Philippa handed me a vanilla whip cupcake, and her gaze ran over me. "Whatever's the matter with you?"

"What makes you think something's wrong?" I asked.

She waved a hand at me. "You're all gray looking. There hasn't been another death that I wasn't aware of?"

"Only Blaine Masters' murder," I said. "And you predicted that. Sabine Novak has been taken away by the police. Campbell's certain it was her."

"And it's this murder that's making you so down?" She took a large bite of her cupcake.

My mouth twisted to the side as I pulled off a piece of cupcake and fed it to Meatball. "It's mainly that."

"Go on, Holly, no secrets. Something else is troubling you."

I glanced up to see her steady gaze on me. I needed to confide in someone. "I'm having a few problems with Lord Rupert. Not problems exactly. I think he's fond of me."

"And are you fond of him?"

"I am. I value his friendship."

"That's good. A long lasting relationship has to have that firm foundation. And what else?"

"You wouldn't mind if Rupert and I dated?"

"I think you're both fine people."

"Even though I work in the kitchen and he's nobility?"

"That's semantics."

I was glad that was cleared up.

"Spit it out, girl. That's not the only thing on your mind," Lady Philippa said.

"I may have the offer of a new job."

The cupcake she was lifting to her mouth stopped moving. "You're thinking of leaving?"

"I wasn't. I love my job here. I love everything about the castle, the village, and the people. But Chef Heston doesn't care if I stay or go."

Lady Philippa shook her head as she started eating her cupcake again. "What about Campbell?"

"What about him?"

"I see him talking to you. He values your input in these investigations."

I snorted a laugh. "He definitely doesn't. Campbell tells me to keep my nose out and back off. He's always catching me talking to people when I shouldn't be. He'll be another one who's glad when I go."

"If you go," Lady Philippa said. She finished her cupcake and licked her fingers. She pulled out two dog biscuits and fed them to the dogs. "There's no need for you to go anywhere. Let's deal with your problems. Campbell's a typical alpha male. He has to be right. There's no negotiating that. Even if he's wrong, he'll argue that he's right until he's exhausted everyone and they simply agree with him."

"How do I deal with that?" I asked. "Sometimes, I feel like I'm banging my head against a brick wall when I talk to him. One minute, he's asking for advice and the next he's telling me to stay away."

"Again, a typical alpha who doesn't want to admit he needs help. The solution to that problem is to make him think he's always right. It doesn't matter if you know otherwise. You'll know the truth, and that's the most important thing. And, if it solves murders and keeps the castle safe, who cares how Campbell behaves?"

"You want me to butter Campbell up and tell him how wonderful he is even when he's wrong?"

"I do. Make him think he's the cat's pajamas. A bit of sweet talking and flattery from you, and he won't know what's hit him."

I shook my head. "I can't do that. I'm terrible at sweet talking. And I won't tell him he's right if he's chasing the wrong suspect. What if an innocent person goes to prison because Campbell's ego gets in the way?"

"I don't see that happening," Lady Philippa said. "I predict Campbell will be here for a long time. As will you.

Your relationship with Campbell will always be on the prickly side, but deep down, he values you, even though he pretends you're an annoyance."

"I guess I can handle not rubbing his nose in it when he gets things wrong," I said.

"You can maybe rub his nose in it now and again." Lady Philippa chuckled. "Just for entertainment's sake. Now, on to Rupert. He's a gentle soul, but a dolt when it comes to being open about his feelings. I'm aware that he's fond of you."

"What do I do with that? We move in different social circles. I'm working in the kitchen at a castle that he may own one day. The differences are too extreme."

"Remove the difficulties for a second. Do you care for him?"

"I think very highly of him," I said. "I value his friendship."

"But nothing more?"

I paused before answering. There was an attraction there. Rupert wasn't your typical gorgeous model type. He could be clumsy and made a fair few gaffes, but he was kind, sweet, and he made me laugh. Wasn't that what every woman wanted?

Lady Philippa leaned forward and tapped my knee. "Follow your heart. True love will find a way if it's meant to be. I understand that it can be difficult. There are expectations set for Rupert in regard to who he'll marry."

"It won't be someone working in a kitchen making cakes," I said. And that was the biggest problem when it came to a relationship with Rupert. He was a Lord. And while I was great, I was a kitchen assistant.

"Now we've solved those problems," Lady Philippa said, "what about this murder?"

I was glad she thought everything was sorted. "The murder is solved."

"Are you sure about that?"

I glanced at the notepad beside Lady Philippa. "Do your predictions suggest otherwise?"

"I'm more interested in what you're thinking. Did Sabine do it?"

I tucked Meatball in the space next to me on the chair and clasped my hands together. "When she was taken away by the police, I didn't feel glad. I'm usually so certain when the real killer has been found. Everything fits. And it should fit here as well. Sabine lied about her alibi, she was Blaine's secret girlfriend, and she'd convinced herself she could be more. Blaine must have had other ideas. It makes sense that it was her."

"Everything points to Sabine, but your gut is telling you otherwise," Lady Philippa said. "Mine's the same. I've not felt settled for days."

"Campbell's convinced that Sabine did it. He's discounted all the other suspects."

"And do we think that Campbell is always right?" Lady Philippa arched an eyebrow.

I couldn't help but smile, despite my muddy thoughts. "I need to keep looking into this, don't I?"

"You already know the answer to that."

I nodded. "Did you know that Henrietta was considered a suspect by Campbell before Sabine was arrested?"

"That's nonsense," Lady Philippa said. "When there is unrest in the castle, I can never sleep. I was up using my binoculars that night. I saw Henrietta outside. She can't have done it."

I blew out a breath. "That's such a relief."

"A member of my family would never be tied up in anything so seedy. Scrub her off the list. I'll be her alibi. But you do need to take another look at this and figure it out. I'm exhausted, and I won't rest easy until this murder is solved."

"It won't do any harm to take another look at the remaining suspects," I said. "Maybe something has been missed."

"And it also wouldn't do any harm to prove Campbell wrong," Lady Philippa said. "Of course, in a delicate way, so his alpha male ego doesn't get bruised."

I grinned. Lady Philippa was right. I wasn't giving up on any of this, not just yet. There were solutions to all my problems. I just needed to find them.

Chapter 17

I pushed the recently repaired delivery bike back into the storage shed and secured it before closing the door. I'd made four deliveries this morning, and I had yet to start on making the cakes for the castle café. I'd have to get a move on if I was going to get everything ticked off my to-do list today.

After my talk with Lady Philippa the previous evening, I felt calmer and more settled than I had done for days. It was always good to talk through problems with friends.

"Time to get you in your …" I looked around. Meatball had vanished.

"Where are you hiding?" I walked back to the shed and double-checked that I hadn't shut him in there.

I walked onto the main path and spotted his furry little behind scampering toward the family's private garden.

He'd most likely gotten a sniff of the Duchess's corgis and was off to investigate, see if he could pick a fight and show them who was the boss in small dog land.

The Duchess wouldn't mind if Meatball blundered into her garden, but I didn't have time to chase after him this morning.

I jogged behind him and caught him as he stopped to sniff an alluring smell next to a bush.

Just as I'd scooped him up, voices drifted toward me. I recognized the Duchess's voice immediately, and I was pretty sure the other one was Percy.

I turned to sneak away, not wanting to intrude, but then stopped as I caught the end of a sentence.

"She's not the woman I thought she was," Percy said, his voice low.

Was he talking about his wife, Diana? I adjusted Meatball to make him more comfortable in my arms and remained hidden by the bush.

"People change over time," the Duchess said. "It's important to be flexible in a marriage. Everyone's partners have their little quirks."

"That's part of the problem. Diana has never grown up. I mean no disrespect to your daughter. When we first got together, I loved her vivaciousness. I've always liked the quiet life, but Diana helped to bring out my fun side."

"She has always enjoyed a party," the Duchess said.

"I keep suggesting we try different things. Things we can do as a couple. Things that don't involve going out drinking and dancing, but she's not interested. And ... I was hoping we'd start a family soon."

"I would welcome grandchildren."

"Every time I suggest the idea, she laughs and tells me she's far too young to be a mother. But I'm ready to have a family. What if Diana never is? I want to be a father."

"Have you spoken to her? Marriages work better if there's open dialog."

"I've lost count of the number of times I've tried. She's more interested in updating her social media accounts than having a sensible conversation with her husband." There was a short pause. "I don't want to burden you with this, but—"

"I asked you if there was a problem. I sensed the other morning that things weren't well between you two. I don't like to think of my children being unhappy. I spoke to Diana, and she said everything was perfect. Which is why I pulled you aside this morning. Mothers always know when something is wrong."

"It's been getting worse over the last year. The more I push her into making a home for our future children, the more she goes out and parties. I asked her if she was scared about the prospect of becoming a mother, but she brushed it off. Diana said she'd hire a nanny and be done with it. But that's not how I want our children to be raised. I want both of us to be in their lives. That's important."

"I agree," the Duchess said. "I did employ a nanny when I had my children, but I was always there for them. It's important you're around when your children are growing up."

"I get the impression Diana wants to continue with her party lifestyle even after we have a family."

"Perhaps a little space would do you both good. You could pursue your own hobbies. Diana may realize what she has when you aren't always around."

"I've been doing that in a way. I was spending a lot of time with Blaine before he, well, we all know what happened."

I'd been intending to tiptoe away until I heard Blaine's name mentioned.

"Blaine lived on the extreme end of the single life," Percy said. "He was all about the good times, just like Diana. I sometimes wondered if the two of them would have been better off together."

"No, Diana was never meant for someone like Blaine. She needs you in her life. You're her steadying influence."

"What if I don't want to be her steadying influence anymore?" Percy asked. "Blaine made me forget my worries, and we had fun together."

"What kind of fun are we talking about?" The Duchess's tone sharpened.

"Nothing bad! Although I get the impression Diana was worried that Blaine was leading me astray, but he wasn't. I'm not interested in any other woman. I've met the woman I want to spend my life with, but she doesn't always make it easy."

I cuddled Meatball against me. So that was the reason Percy had been spending time with Blaine before he'd died. He was in an unhappy marriage and didn't know what to do about it. That would explain why he'd been so shifty when we all had breakfast together.

"Even so, Blaine Masters may have not been giving you the best advice when it comes to your relationship," the Duchess said.

Percy chuckled. "He gave terrible relationship advice. I never listened to it. He told me to avoid getting tied down, but that's what I wanted. I've never been one to play the field. When I met Diana, I just knew she was right for me. And we were happy for the first few years, but things have slowly gone downhill. I'm not sure how much longer I can take it, especially now Blaine's gone. He was my escape. He wouldn't ask questions or tell me I was doing anything wrong. I got a bit of teasing, but I could handle that. I'm not sure what I'm going to do now."

"I am sorry your friend has gone. And I suspect I make a substandard second choice, but I'm always here if you need to talk. Even though Diana is my daughter, I won't judge you. I've been married to the Duke for a long time, and he's not always the easiest of men. I understand the need for finding your own personal refuge when things get difficult."

"Thanks. When you brought me out here this morning, I thought you were going to yell at me, and that Diana had told you things were going wrong and it was all my fault."

"I find that yelling doesn't get you very far," the Duchess said.

"Maybe I'm just not handling things well. What with Blaine being killed by Sabine, I'm still in shock. Everyone knew he had a wild side when it came to women, but I never thought it would end like this. I figured he'd eventually find someone who'd make him want to settle and marry."

"Most men do find a suitable woman," the Duchess said. "I'm terribly sorry for your loss."

"I just wish Sabine would confess to what she did. It's only making it harder that she's denying being involved," Percy said. "The police are running DNA tests to see if they can get any evidence to pin her to the murder, but I'm not sure what the tests will prove. They were together; her DNA will be somewhere on Blaine."

"They haven't formally charged her yet?" the Duchess asked. "When I spoke with my head of security, he said the case was as good as closed."

I shook my head. Typical Campbell doing his 'I'm always right' thing. Maybe he only said that to the Duchess to ensure she didn't worry, but he was jumping the gun, especially if Sabine had yet to confess.

"It's only a matter of time," Percy said. "Have you seen Sabine's online posts about weddings and hinting that she'd soon be married to Blaine? The woman was out of her mind. He'd never have married her. If he was going to marry anyone, it would have been Lila. She comes from the right background. She fit his social circle. And she tolerated his cheating."

"Ah, I don't really do social media," the Duchess said. "We have a team in the castle who handle the mystifying tweeting and updates. I still enjoy having an actual conversation on the phone."

"I don't blame you for staying away from it. If you did see it, you'd be shocked. Sabine was obsessed with Blaine. That wasn't healthy. Maybe there were warning signs that she was going to do something like this, but none of us noticed. Blaine always joked that she was madly in love with him."

"I'm sure Campbell and the police will soon have this tidied up," the Duchess said. "Now, I have a few suggestions about what to do with Diana to help iron out these wrinkles in your relationship."

I took that as my cue to leave, sliding my phone out of my back pocket as I hurried back to my apartment.

I set Meatball on the floor once we were inside and made us both a quick breakfast—toast for me, kibble for him—as I scrolled through Sabine's Instagram account.

Percy hadn't been exaggerating. Her page was full of pictures of wedding dresses, wedding venues, and even pictures of cake. And there was a liberal scattering of the initials BM among them. It didn't take a genius to work out who she wanted to get married to.

As I kept scrolling through Sabine's post, I kept finding #nopoo. What was that?

I opened a browser page and typed it in. It turned out that #nopoo had nothing to do with a sensitive digestive issue, it was all about not shampooing your hair.

That couldn't be good for your scalp. Surely, you needed to wash the grease and dirt off, especially if you exercised or had to go cycling several times a week up and down hills pulling large loads of cake.

I returned to Sabine's page and kept scrolling.

Six months of #nopoo #glossylocks

It's my #nopoo anniversary. Doesn't my hair look incredible?

There were pictures of her hair. Despite being grossed out at the thought of not washing your hair for six months, hers looked amazing. It was thick, glossy, and in perfect condition.

My toast fell from my hand, and I stood up. Sabine didn't wash her hair! Even when she showered, she got no water on it. Having had a read of one of the webpages, I knew how important it was to make sure your hair never got wet or you'd undo the progress you made with your no shampooing mission.

"Which means she's innocent," I said out loud. She could have been telling the truth. Sabine could have been in the shower on the night of Blaine's murder.

"Woof woof?" Meatball looked up at me from his empty food bowl.

"I have to tell Campbell about this," I said. "They're going to charge the wrong person with murder."

Chapter 18

I raced out the door of my apartment and tucked Meatball in his kennel before striding away in search of Campbell.

I'd had no idea that such a thing as not shampooing your hair existed, but it was plastered all over Sabine's Instagram page. This new information weakened the case against her.

Campbell would be less than happy when I told him about this, but I couldn't keep it to myself. I'd handle his complaints about my snooping, but I couldn't let a criminal get away with murder. And that's exactly what would happen if Sabine was charged with Blaine's murder.

I turned the corner and spotted Saracen marching away from the castle. I raced over to him. "Wait up! I'm looking for Campbell."

He turned and lifted a hand in greeting. "Hey, Holly. You'll find him at the shooting range this morning."

Oh, boy! I didn't want to be around Campbell when he had a gun in his hand, especially not when I was about to deliver bad news. "He's shooting at things?"

"That's what you tend to do on a shooting range." Saracen grinned at me. "What's up?"

"I've got something to tell him that he won't be happy about."

"Then make sure he doesn't aim his gun at you," Saracen said. "Campbell never misses his target."

I gulped. "That's good to know. Oh, and I've got some new cookies for you to try. Zero sugar and they taste great." I was already backing away from Saracen, my thoughts on how to break the news to Campbell without him shooting at me.

"I look forward to trying them," he said.

I raced away from the castle and along the gravel driveway. The shooting range was near the archery site where I'd seen Rupert and James the other morning.

Shots rang out as I jogged along a narrow tree-lined path. I slowed as I came to a clearing.

Large trees surrounded the range, and distant targets were set against a high bank of earth and sandbags.

Campbell stood with his legs apart. He was dressed head to toe in black and wore ear protectors as he fired at a target that looked a bit fuzzy to me from this distance.

I waited for him to stop firing, then tapped him on the shoulder.

He flinched before turning and arching an eyebrow. He pulled off his ear protectors. "You're here to practice?"

I shook my head. "No, those things will kill you."

He didn't smile. "That's the plan. Why are you here?"

"I have to tell you about no poo," I said.

Campbell's gaze flickered over me. "Try prune juice."

"What? No, this isn't about me."

"A strong coffee and a jog usually works as well." He changed the clip in his gun. "But if you're sick, go to the doctor. I only have basic medical training."

"No! Listen to me. No poo. Hashtag no poo."

"You can say it to me as many times as you like, you're still not making any sense. Prune juice, coffee, and a run.

That'll see you right."

"It's a hashtag used online. It's about people not washing their hair. No shampoo. Shortened to no poo."

"Yeah, thanks for that exciting bit of news, but I don't need to worry about my hair. I get a buzz cut every other week."

"I'm not talking about your hair. Sabine doesn't wash her hair."

He turned to face me. "Ever?"

"It's all over her social media accounts. There's this trend going around that if you don't wash your hair for long enough, it starts to self-clean."

He grunted and shook his head. "This has to be a joke."

"No joke. I couldn't believe it either when I read about it on her page, but it's true. Sabine never washes her hair. Which means—"

"We're going to have to let her go." Campbell sighed as he holstered his gun.

"She may still be guilty," I said, "but she didn't lie about her alibi. She could have been in the shower when Blaine was killed. And if no one checked her bathroom that night, there's no way to know if she used the shower."

He rubbed his forehead. "I'm not surprised to hear this. Well, I am surprised people don't wash their hair. That's just nasty. But we weren't getting anywhere with the physical evidence. And Sabine keeps saying she's innocent. I've gone over her story a dozen times and it stays the same. Usually, when a person's lying, they eventually slip up. She hasn't slipped once."

"If it's any consolation, I thought she was good for the murder too. She fits perfectly, but without evidence—"

"She's a free woman." Campbell ran a hand down his face. "I already agreed with the police to have her released, and this new bit of information adds to my belief that the killer is still on the loose."

My phone pinged, and I pulled it out of my pocket. "Um, we may have a problem. How long has Sabine been out for?"

"Less than an hour. Why?"

"I set up an alert every time she posted something new online. Her latest posts talk about being falsely accused by the police, suing, and discrimination."

"Let me see that." He grabbed my phone and looked at the posts before hissing out air through his teeth. "We're discriminating against her because she's too pretty according to this rubbish."

I took the phone back. There were several hashtags, including one that read #tooprettytobeimprisoned.

"This woman is unbelievable. She won't get anywhere trying to sue us," Campbell said. "We had grounds to hold her."

"Not anymore," I said.

His fingers flexed, and his eyes flashed a warning. "I told her not to say anything. She agreed to keep quiet until we'd re-interviewed the other suspects. We need to keep this on the down low so we don't alert the actual killer."

"Do you think they'll make a run for it? You could get your team watching for anyone acting suspiciously."

"Thanks for the advice."

"Hey! I didn't have to tell you any of this. I'm—"

"Helping. I know." He scraped a hand across his chin. "Who do you think did it?"

I pressed my lips together to stop from smiling. "Are you asking for my help to solve this murder?"

"I didn't say that," he said. "I'll figure this out."

"Maybe you'll figure it out a bit quicker if I'm assisting you."

His hand rested on the butt of his gun, and I took a step back. Maybe I shouldn't tease the enormous former superspy when he had a huge gun strapped to him.

"What are you thinking, Holmes?" he said. "Go on, Little Miss Sleuth. Let me hear your theories."

I gathered my thoughts before nodding. "We can discount Sabine."

"Already done."

"And you can also scrub Henrietta Audley off your list. Lady Philippa saw her out walking when Blaine's body was discovered. Her alibi holds up."

"You don't think Lady Philippa is covering for her?"

"No, she wouldn't do that. Even though they're related, she wouldn't let a killer go free."

"Anyone else we can lose from the list?"

"I'm still not certain about Percy or Lady Diana. Percy was spending time with Blaine because his marriage is in trouble. Would he kill the person who gave him a time out from his problems?"

"How do you know they're having problems?"

I tilted my head from side to side. "I may have overheard something when I was passing by."

"You were eavesdropping."

"You do it."

"Prove it."

"Anyway, it doesn't matter how I know. I don't think it was Percy, but maybe Lady Diana was unhappy with Blaine. She could have confronted him about the amount of time he spent with Percy."

He shook his head. "She's a lightweight. More concerned with her public image than anything else. A murder on her hands would seriously dent her reputation. Who else?"

"There's only Lila. She doesn't have a good alibi. She was alone in bed."

"She was also after Blaine for his money," Campbell said. "Would she kill her golden goose?"

"Lila could have lost her temper," I said. "I wouldn't be happy if my boyfriend brought his secret girlfriend to a party we were going to. I may even have been inclined to shove him down the stairs."

"I didn't know you were so ruthless," he said. "I'll make sure I watch my back."

"If I tried to shove you down the stairs, you wouldn't even move," I said. "Not even if I used a baseball bat."

"I may flinch at that. But you'd have to get close enough to swing it first." His eyes narrowed. "Have you ever thought about doing that to me?"

"Only once or twice," I said.

"Huh! It's possible Lila followed Blaine after he left their bedroom. She could have woken up when he slipped out."

"Or she faked being asleep, knowing he'd sneak off and see Sabine."

"That's also possible."

"And she knew about their relationship. Sabine's been indiscreet online. Lila could have followed Blaine, surprised him at the top of the stairs, and shoved him. She then hurried back to her room before the guard found the body at the bottom of the stairs."

"Then that's the next move," Campbell said. "I bring Lila in for more questioning and see if anything shakes loose. It's a good motive."

"I'm glad to have helped." I beamed at him.

He grunted. "I bet you are."

I checked my watch. "I need to get back to work. Even though I may not have a job here for much longer, I still have a lot to keep me busy."

Campbell cocked his head. "What does that mean?"

I lifted my hand. "Nothing. I meant, my job solving crime. I've had enough of all this snooping around."

"Sure you have. You'll be solving crimes when you're a wizened old lady with a hunchback."

"I intend to age gracefully. I won't have a hunchback."

He grabbed my shoulders and yanked them back. "You will if you don't sort out that posture."

I rolled my shoulders. Maybe I hunched a little. "So, how can I help with questioning Lila?"

"I'll bring her in. If she causes me problems, I'll call in the big guns."

"I'm a big gun?"

"In your dreams. You're a water pistol. Stick to what you're good at."

"Solving crime?"

"Baking. You love the kitchen." He raised a hand before I had a chance to protest. "Don't think I'm not appreciating your input at this stage, but I'll do the next step alone."

I tugged on my bottom lip as Campbell walked away, a little peeved not to be included. Still, Campbell had a point. He was the superspy, and I was the super baker. The castle kitchen had always felt like a home away from home, but I had the little problem of Lorcan trying to poach me.

I may be able to solve murders, but I wasn't sure what I was going to do about my future at Audley Castle.

❦❦❦❦❦❦ ❦❦❦❦❦❦

I stood back with a smile on my face as I looked at all the ticks beside my to-do list. My work was done in the kitchen for the day. It had been so busy that I'd not given much thought to who killed Blaine and how Campbell was getting on.

He must have brought Lila in for questioning by now. Maybe he'd solved the murder this time, and the right person would be charged.

I pulled out my phone, which I'd been checking all day, as Sabine kept updating her social media accounts. Every post was about the injustice of her arrest and the things she was going to do to make sure her name was cleared. They often involved suing and getting compensation. Sabine always had her eye on the money prize.

"Walk time," I called as I headed to Meatball's kennel.

He bounced out, danced around my feet, and waited as I put his leash on.

As I walked away from the castle toward the trees, I kept scrolling through Sabine's accounts. Even just a day of looking at social media, and I wasn't feeling great about myself. Everyone looked so stunning online. They had perfect bodies, amazing makeup, and their hair was too good to be true. Maybe it was. I knew a little about adding filters that altered your appearance, but could you really change yourself so much to look that perfect?

I pulled a large piece of pecan, maple syrup, and triple chocolate flapjack from my pocket and ate it. I'd take sweet treats and a few extra pounds any day over perfection. Maybe I should create a hashtag to reflect that. It could be something like #realandlovingcake.

I shoved my phone back in my pocket. Social media wasn't for me.

I glanced over my shoulder, pausing to admire the castle as it stood bathed in the late evening sunshine.

Maybe I should consider a makeover. A few tweaks around the edges to improve myself.

I wasn't thinking about lip fillers or new hairstyles, but Lorcan Blaze's job offer was still on my mind. Would taking it improve my job prospects? Although I wasn't certain how serious he'd been when we'd spoken about it. Serious enough to ask for a reference from Chef Heston.

I took my phone out again and brought up his website and social media accounts. I spent the next half an hour engaging in some serious cake porn. His pursuit of perfection had won him numerous awards, and he'd been featured in magazines across the world, many of the articles discussing his stunning wedding cakes.

Lorcan knew what he was doing when it came to making beautiful cakes. My stomach growled in appreciation as I admired the triple layer frosted cakes, pastel pink cakes covered in flowers, sparkling glitter cakes, tower cakes, and cookie stacks.

I wasn't the only one who thought he made amazing cakes. He had an enormous following online. Over three million people on Instagram, including a number of celebrities. If I worked with him, I'd be moving in impressive social circles, and I'd really get to stretch my skills.

I lowered my phone. What would it be like working for Lorcan? I was used to being yelled at by Chef Heston, but his yelling was because he expected excellence. And he did have a softer side, which he brought out once or twice a year.

It was Lorcan's massive ego I had an issue with. I wasn't certain I wanted to work for a man who abandoned a woman by the roadside when she needed help.

As I kept checking through his accounts, I couldn't find any posts older than five years. Maybe he didn't do social media before that.

I did a general search on Lorcan's background and how he rose to fame, but couldn't get much information. There was a general information page on his website about his training and experience, but it was vague. It was almost as if he didn't exist until recently.

I put my phone away and finished the walk with Meatball before circling back to my apartment.

Once Meatball was settled on his bed with a fresh bowl of water and a new chew toy, I grabbed the cookies I'd promised Saracen and headed to his apartment. Maybe he could help me learn more about Lorcan's background. If I was thinking about working for him, I needed to know everything I could. I had to be prepared for whatever he'd throw at me.

I knocked on Saracen's door, and he opened it a few seconds later. His gaze went to the plate of cookies in my hand and he licked his lips. "I've been dreaming about cookies."

"Then your dreams have been answered. I've done a different mix of fruit, and there are dates in these as well. Zero refined sugar. You can probably get away with two or three after a meal if you're careful. Although make sure you test your blood sugars. I don't want you collapsing on me again."

"Sure thing, Mom." He gestured me into his apartment. "And your timing is perfect. I've just had dinner and definitely have room for dessert. Join me."

"Thanks. Actually, I have an ulterior motive for being here."

Saracen was already munching on a cookie as he walked into his kitchen. "What's that?"

"Are you able to trace someone's history for me?"

"I sure can. Who are you stalking?" Saracen grinned at me. "Great cookies."

"I'm not stalking anyone. It's just that, well, I've been offered a rare opportunity, but I'm not sure about the person who offered it to me."

He gestured to a seat, and I sat down. "Interesting. Who is this person making you an offer you can't refuse so long as he checks out?"

"The baker hired to make the anniversary cake at the party. Lorcan Blaze."

Saracen snorted a laugh as he set to work on his second cookie. "That's got to be a false name. Who'd call their kid that?"

"I think it's his real name. The weird thing is, I can't find any information about him that's older than five years old. It's like he didn't exist before then."

Saracen set the plate of cookies on the table and opened his laptop. "Let's see what this guy's hiding. You can make the drinks if you like. This will take a few minutes."

While Saracen did his spy thing on the computer, I made us tea before settling back in my seat and taking a cookie.

"This is fascinating," Saracen said. "Lorcan Blaze hasn't always been called Lorcan Blaze."

"He changed his name?"

"He used to be called Matthew Hallsworth. And you're right, Lorcan Blaze suddenly appeared five years ago."

"Maybe he changed his name because he wanted to make sure people remembered him."

"It's certainly hard to forget a name like that," Saracen said. "And it's worked. He's got a huge following online."

I nodded. "Can you do a search for Matthew Hallsworth?"

"What's the offer this guy's made you?" Saracen tapped away on the keyboard as he spoke.

I bit my bottom lip. I wasn't sure how ready I was to discuss this. "Lorcan runs a chain of successful patisseries and restaurants. He's always looking out for talent to add to his team."

Saracen's fingers paused, and he glanced up. "You're thinking of leaving?"

"Not for certain. But he's made me an offer. I want to know what I'll be walking into if I take it."

Saracen's bottom lip jutted out. "Who'll make me my treats if you go?"

I chuckled. "We do have a very talented chef in the castle's kitchen."

"Who spends most of his time being grumpier than Campbell," Saracen said. "Don't tell me I have to learn to bake for myself. The last time I made cookies, I set them on fire by mistake."

"It's just a possibility that I might be leaving," I said. "And if I do go, we can have a few tries at making cookies together. You'll be an expert by the time I leave."

"You shouldn't leave," Saracen said. "That would solve the problem."

I sighed. It might solve one problem, but it would leave me with several more.

"Okay, there's not much on Matthew Hallsworth from an early age, but he's definitely the same guy," Saracen said. "He started out as a kitchen hand, then went on to be a sous chef, and then a junior chef. He worked his way through several kitchens."

"That's a typical career path for someone looking to get into the trade," I said. "Do you have any pictures of him?"

"Not many. There are no social media accounts opened in his old name. There are a few pictures, though." Saracen shifted the laptop so I could see.

"I don't see Lorcan in any of these." I pointed at the screen. "But look, that's Blaine Masters in the center of this picture. I'd recognize that smug face anywhere."

Saracen leaned over to take a look. "So it is. The dead guy and Lorcan knew each other?"

I shook my head. "No, Lorcan's not in this picture."

"Let me zoom in. Maybe he's at the back."

I scanned the faces once the image had been blown up, looking at them several times. "Maybe Blaine knew a different Matthew Hallsworth. It's not such an unusual name." I squinted at the screen, trying to pick Lorcan out. He could have a different hairstyle or facial hair, but no one in that picture looked anything like him.

"Any luck?"

I peered at an arm on the edge of the photograph. "Can you enhance this bit?" I pointed at the arm.

"Sure." Saracen did his magic before passing the laptop back to me.

I inhaled sharply. "I've seen that tattoo before. That's Lorcan Blaze's arm at the edge of the picture. He did know Blaine. When was this picture taken?"

"Six years ago," Saracen said. "Is that important?"

I sat in silence for a few seconds. Blaine knew Lorcan when he was called Matthew. Had something bad happened between them? Something that meant Matthew Hallsworth needed to become Lorcan Blaze.

"Holly, you're sort of creeping me out. You're staring into space and muttering to yourself," Saracen said.

I jumped up from my seat. "Thanks, Saracen. You've been a big help."

"No problem. Does this mean you've made a decision about staying at the castle?"

"Oh, I've definitely made a decision. I'm going to speak to Lorcan right away about his offer."

But first of all, I had to ask him about what happened between him and Blaine all those years ago.

Chapter 19

My heart pounded so hard that I felt dizzy as I reached Lorcan's bedroom door. I sucked in a deep breath and knocked.

"Who is it?"

"It's Holly. I've come to talk to you about the job offer."

"Come in."

I entered the room to discover Lorcan sitting up in bed. He looked clean, recently shaved, and no longer gray. There was a tray by the side of his bed with an empty plate on it. "You're getting your appetite back?"

"I'm recovering," he said. "So, you've come to your senses. I knew you'd take me up on the offer. You're fortunate that I'm still here. I plan to leave today."

Then my timing couldn't have been better. "I am interested in your offer. My boss has made it clear he doesn't want me around. I won't stay where I'm not wanted."

"More fool him. We'll reap the rewards of your desserts together." A smug smile crossed Lorcan's face. "I can make you a star."

"That sounds great." I walked closer to the bed. "I'd love to know how you got started in your career."

"That's not important," Lorcan said. "Where I am now is the only thing that matters. The success I've generated will brush off on you."

"I hope it will. Where did you train?"

"Several places. What about you?"

"I did a part-time course at the local college while getting hands-on experience in a few cafés," I said. "The theory part of baking is important, but I don't think you can beat making desserts and having people try them."

"I agree. Catering college can only teach you so much. It wasn't until I got in the real world that I made a name for myself."

"You must have worked for some important people over the years."

"Of course I have. There's a three-month waiting list at my restaurant, and my patisseries are always busy. I'm opening three more in the next six months. You're joining at the right time. How do you like the idea of Dubai?"

"I'm sure that would be amazing. I'd love to hear about the celebrities you've baked for, though."

"You'll get your chance to meet some for yourself, if you play your cards right." He smoothed a hand through his hair. "Let's just say most of the A-listers in Hollywood have me on speed dial. I'm often picked up in a private jet and taken to the most exclusive parties in the world to provide the catering. You can be involved with that if you're as good as you think you are."

"You've tasted my desserts. You know I can bake."

"Your journey is just beginning. But don't think this will be an easy ride. You'll have to work your way up, earn your stripes the same as everyone else. While you do that, you'll get to see the world. And I pay my staff well. I work my teams hard and I expect top-class results, but it'll all be worth it."

"That sounds exciting," I said.

"Of course, you have to leave all this behind." He waved a hand in the air. "I'm hoping you don't have children or an annoying boyfriend who'll get in the way."

"No children or boyfriend," I said. "I do have a dog."

"A dog can't come with you."

My gut twisted as I forced a smile. I'd never leave Meatball behind. "That won't be a problem."

"Good. I need your total commitment to this job. You'll be on call twenty-four hours a day, seven days a week. My clients have exacting needs and often call at the last minute. It's important we're accommodating."

I hated the idea of that. These clients needed to get better at planning their parties. "Whatever you need."

Lorcan's gaze ran over me before he nodded. "Welcome aboard. I'm gathering your references, but that's a formality. It's what you produced in the kitchen that made the most impact on me."

"Chef Heston has received the reference request from you," I said. "He wasn't happy about it."

"Because he knows what he's losing."

I couldn't let his flattery distract me, although it felt good to be wanted. "I believe you worked with Blaine Masters a few years ago."

Lorcan sucked in a breath before shaking his head. "No, I didn't know him. What makes you say that?"

"Someone may have mentioned it to me," I said. "Did you cater for one of his parties?"

"You've gotten it wrong. Who's spreading these rumors?" He clenched the sheets in his fists. "Tell me now."

"I don't remember," I said. "It's not true?"

Lorcan didn't speak for several seconds, his chest rising and falling rapidly.

I was onto something. Lorcan had worked for Blaine. This couldn't be a coincidence.

"You shouldn't listen to gossip," Lorcan finally said.

"I never do, but you must have been shocked to hear he was dead," I said.

"I imagine everyone was shocked, but I never met the guy. I've been sick in bed all this time. I didn't meet any of the party guests."

"Perhaps you catered for him when you were called Matthew Hallsworth?"

His mouth opened and closed several times, but he didn't speak.

"That was your old name, wasn't it?"

Lorcan's face drained of color. "I'm going to be sick. You should leave. I'm still not well from the food poisoning." He pulled himself off the bed and raced to the bathroom.

I waited by the side of the bed. Lorcan was lying about a lot of things. If he had food poisoning, he'd be over it by now. He shouldn't still be throwing up. He wasn't sick because of poorly cooked food. He was worried that I'd discovered the truth about him.

He returned to the bedroom a moment later, his hands shaking as he sat on the edge of the bed. "I've made a mistake about you. I'm withdrawing my offer of employment."

"Oh! Did I say something wrong?"

"You're too nosy for your own good," he said. "My clients demand discretion. I can imagine if you catered a party, you'd end up poking around in the closets and nosing through private correspondence. I've met your type before. You can't be trusted. You always have to dig and find out things that aren't important."

"This seems important to you," I said. "Why did you change your name?"

Lorcan glared at me, his lips pressed together. "I don't feel so good." He dropped back on the bed and covered his eyes with his hand.

"I'll get you some water." I hurried into the bathroom and filled a glass I found on the side. I was turning away from the sink when I saw a prescription medicine bottle on the counter. I picked it up and read the label. Cordarone.

"What you doing in there?" Lorcan said.

"Nothing." A warning on the medicine bottle said *may cause vomiting*.

I placed the bottle down. Lorcan could have used these drugs to fake his illness. He made himself sick so he couldn't complete the job on the anniversary cake.

I swallowed down my panic, my mouth going dry. Had he set this whole thing up? Lorcan needed to get access to the party so he could get to Blaine. He knew that Blaine would be here, and this was the only way he could get through the door and reach him.

I walked back to the bedroom and handed him the glass of water.

Lorcan took a sip. "Leave now. I was wrong about you. You're an average baker. You're not good enough for my team."

"I'm more than good enough." I placed my hands on my hips. "You faked your food poisoning."

"You can't fake food poisoning," he said.

"There are drugs in your bathroom that induce vomiting."

"That's one of the side effects," he said. "But that medication is for my heart condition. I have an irregular heartbeat."

"I don't believe you," I said.

"Then check with my doctor," Lorcan said. "He'll confirm I have a problem, but it's treatable with that medication."

"You knew Blaine Masters," I said. "What did he do to you that was so bad that you changed your name and reinvented yourself?"

Lorcan set his glass down, closed his eyes, and rubbed the palms of his hands against them. "How did you find out?"

"I saw a picture of you at a party with Blaine. You were right on the edge of the photo."

He lowered his hands and shook his head. "I've changed my look. Different hair, fixed my teeth, even had a nose job. I look nothing like Matthew. You can't have recognized me."

"Your tattoos haven't changed," I said. "You still have the sleeve of tattoos."

Lorcan scowled as he rubbed a hand up his arm. "I should have gotten them removed. I try not to let people see them because they're so distinctive. You really picked me out of the photo because of the tattoos on my arm?"

I shrugged. "As you said, I'm nosy. I poke around and see things other people miss. What did Blaine do to you?"

Lorcan let out a long sigh. "He ruined me."

"How?"

He stared into space, his eyes narrowing as if he was recalling a disturbing memory. "I was new to the world of celebrity baking. I was in over my head after getting a recommendation from a wealthy stockbroker. I'd catered for his party and it went really well. He spread the word about my services, and the next thing I knew I was inundated with demands. I didn't turn any of them down. It was my chance to make it big, if only I could keep on top of everything. The problem was, it was just me and a part-time assistant. I didn't have time to hire anyone else and train them up."

"You tried to handle all the orders yourself?"

"I got by on four hours of sleep and a gallon of coffee every day for six months. And it worked. But then I made a mistake. I was catering Blaine's birthday party, and the cake went wrong. When he cut into it, it wasn't cooked properly."

"And Blaine told everybody about it?"

"He didn't shut up about what a disaster the party had been because of my food. He threw the cake on the floor in front of everyone and threatened to sue me. That happened just after that picture you saw had been taken. I was so humiliated. Blaine was a big shot. He had influence, and everyone listened to him. After that, the calls stopped, the money vanished, and I lost it all. Before that, I had a great life, an amazing home, a solid gold reputation, and a model for a fiancée. She didn't stick around for long after the money stopped rolling in."

"So, you changed your name, started again, and reinvented yourself as Lorcan Blaze," I said.

His shoulders slumped as he nodded. "I had to do something. Everything I worked so hard for was draining away. It was during that time that I developed my heart problem. The doctor said it was a combination of stress, not sleeping properly, and drinking too much. Blaine made me sick. And I learned the hard way that those drugs made me throw up if I got the dosage even slightly wrong."

"Did you know Blaine would be at this party?"

"I didn't. But fate handed him to me. I almost walked into him not long after I arrived at the castle. I could barely hide my shock. It was the same old smug Blaine, so full of himself and thinking he owned the world." Lorcan's top lip curled. "After I got over my astonishment at seeing him, I realized this was the opportunity I'd been waiting for. Blaine had ruined me, so I decided to do the same to him. He lived a wasteful and extravagant life. He was a cold, shallow man who took what he wanted and discarded anyone who no longer did his bidding. He took pleasure in ruining me."

"You didn't have to kill him, though," I said. "I get that you hated him. I'd have been tempted to spike his food with laxatives if he'd done that to me, but murder!"

He snorted a laugh. "Yeah, that's kindergarten revenge. I wanted Blaine to lose everything, and the only way I could do that was by taking his life. He had to die."

"You faked your food poisoning using your heart medication?" I said.

"That's right. It was easy to do. I'm sensitive to the pills. I knew how much I needed to take to make myself sick. I took the drugs, let them get to work, and then planned my next move." He shifted on the bed, still staring into space. "I figured Blaine wouldn't have changed. He was always one for the women. I saw him with his girlfriend, then saw him with his personal assistant getting up close and friendly when they thought no one was looking. That was all I needed."

"What did you do? Wait outside his bedroom until Blaine slipped off to see Sabine?"

"Pretty much. His room was along the same corridor as mine. I made such a fuss about being unwell that I knew I'd be put in a room out of the way. I was right at the end of the corridor, so it was easy to keep my door open and watch everyone's movements. Once Blaine left his bedroom, I crept out after him."

"And you confronted him at the top of the stairs?"

"It was perfect. Fate definitely gave me a helping hand on that front. Blaine was stumbling around like the drunk idiot he was, giggling to himself and rubbing his hands together. He thought he had it all. I called his name just as he got to the stairs." Lorcan snorted a soft laugh. "He turned around and almost tipped backward without me having to do a thing."

"But he didn't fall?"

Lorcan shook his head. "Blaine didn't recognize me. Even when I revealed my old name, he shrugged it off and told me to get a life. That was it. I'd had enough. I had an incredible life, and despite him taking everything from me, I'd come back stronger and better. I'm glad I did it. I have no regrets."

"How did you know for sure that Blaine was dead after you pushed him?"

"You don't smash down a flight of stone stairs and survive. I stood at the top for several minutes, just looking at him to make sure he didn't get up. I've thought about Blaine Masters every day over the last six years. He's finally gone. He can't mess with anyone else."

"Weren't you worried that someone may have seen you following him?"

"It was late. Everyone was either in bed or too drunk to see straight. I only left when I heard someone approaching from the bottom of the stairs. I just made it back to my room before people started shouting. Of course, they didn't bother to look in on me. They figured the annoying chef with food poisoning wouldn't be a problem. It was the perfect cover." His eyes narrowed as he turned to face me. "At least, it was until you started poking around in my business."

"And the police will start poking around in your business as well," I said. "I can't keep this quiet."

"Of course you can. Name your price," he said. "I'm a wealthy man, I can give you anything you want. You want a job with me, I can give you a decent position. You don't need to work up the ranks. I'll offer you a stunning salary and all the benefits you desire. I'll even provide you with your own apartment."

"I can't work for a killer," I said. "I understand what Blaine did was terrible; he should never have done that to you. But you changed your life and showed him you were the better man. You have this amazing career."

"It wasn't enough," he said. "Not while that sadistic jerk lived. You don't ignore an opportunity like this when it comes your way. Only an idiot would do that."

I took a step toward the door. I had to tell the police. Lorcan had just confessed to murder. He couldn't go free. No matter what tempting offer he presented to me, it would never be enough.

"No, you don't get to leave." Lorcan jumped off the bed and stood in front of the door. "You know my secret. You're the only one alive who does. You're not leaving this room."

"You're going to kill me too? I've done nothing wrong to you." My gaze went to the door, but there was no way I could reach it.

"You seem like a nice person, Holly. Nice but nosy. Sadly, nice people don't survive in this business. You have to step on others to get to the top."

"That's not true," I said. "You work hard and your talent will speak for itself."

"So says the kitchen assistant on a minimum wage." He sneered at me. "I'm offering you everything. You could serve your desserts to kings and queens all over the world. I can give you an incredible life. You just need to keep this a secret."

"And you just need to confess," I said. "Do the right thing."

"I am doing the right thing. I'm looking out for myself. Blaine's gone, and I couldn't feel happier. You're just a fly in the ointment. And you need to go."

I backed away, my heart thundering. A tiny movement behind Lorcan caught my eye. The door to the bedroom had inched open.

I kept my attention on Lorcan as he inched toward me, his eyes blazing with fury and possibly a hint of madness. Blaine had broken him, and despite changing his name and his appearance, he still wasn't fixed on the inside.

"Don't do this," I said, my voice shaky. "Go to the police, tell them you killed Blaine. If you explain everything, they may be lenient on you. Blaine destroyed your life."

The door behind him opened another inch. Campbell was outside. I resisted the urge to scream for help.

"The police won't care about our history," Lorcan said. "They'll see me as a cold-blooded killer. I'm not going to prison for this. Blaine ruined me once. He's not doing it again."

"And now you've ruined him," I said. "You killed him."

Lorcan growled as he lunged at me.

The door behind him burst open. Campbell charged in. Right behind him was Saracen.

Lorcan had half a second to turn before he yelped as he was knocked to the ground by Campbell.

"I've got him," Campbell said to Saracen. "See to Holly."

Saracen nodded and raced over to me, grabbing my shoulders.

I was glad he did. My knees felt so wobbly that I could barely stand.

"You okay, Holly?" he asked.

I gasped in a breath and nodded. "There's your killer. Lorcan killed Blaine."

Chapter 20

My hands shook as I sat at the kitchen table, drinking hot chocolate and replaying everything that had just happened.

The last half an hour had been a blur. Campbell and Saracen had taken charge of Lorcan, who'd been ranting and raging as they'd marched him to the waiting police car and filled in the local officers on the situation.

Once Campbell had checked me over and made sure I wasn't going to faint, he'd insisted I wait in the kitchen until I could be questioned.

The door to the kitchen opened. Alice, Rupert, Percy, and Lady Diana hurried in. They all started talking at once.

I placed my mug down and lifted a hand. "Please, one at a time. I've had a bit of a shock."

Alice wrapped her arms around me. "Did Lorcan really try to kill you?"

I nodded as I returned her hug. "How did you know?"

"Rupert saw the police car. He asked Campbell what was going on." Alice stepped back.

"He wanted me to keep quiet after I found out who Lorcan Blaze really is and his connection to Blaine."

"And Lorcan murdered Blaine?" Percy stood in front of me, his face pale as he shook his head.

I nodded again. "Everyone sit down. I'll fill you in." I took a moment to gather my thoughts as everyone took their seats and sat looking at me.

Alice grabbed my hand and squeezed.

I drew in a deep breath. "I discovered that Lorcan changed his name five years ago. He used to be called Matthew Hallsworth."

"Why would he do that?" Alice asked.

"Give Holly a chance to tell the story," Rupert said.

She glared at him. "I am! I just want to get to the good bit."

"There's not really a good bit when it comes to murder," I said.

"Oh, of course. You know what I mean." Alice jiggled my arm. "Go on, I won't say another word."

I doubted that would happen. "Lorcan had an unfortunate encounter with Blaine. He catered for his birthday party and it went wrong."

"Hang on a second, was that the party where Blaine threw his cake everywhere?" Percy asked.

"That's right. Were you there?" I asked.

"Yes! I don't remember why he did it, though," Percy said.

"Most likely, he was drunk," Lady Diana said.

"He wasn't happy with the cake Lorcan made," I said. "And Blaine made sure he never got to work again. Lorcan lost everything. His fiancée, his money, his home. It sounded like he was destitute."

"And he waited all this time to get revenge?" Percy asked.

"This wasn't planned. It was just unfortunate that he catered this party and Blaine was also here," I said. "Lorcan never got past the fact that Blaine ruined his life."

"So he decided to destroy his life," Rupert said. "But Lorcan was sick. How did he manage it?"

"He made himself sick," I said. "I discovered heart medication in his bathroom. Take too much, and it makes you unwell. He used that so everyone would believe he was genuinely sick, which took him out of the equation. Nobody would suspect a man with food poisoning of shoving someone down the stairs."

"Oh, dear. I feel responsible," Percy said. "We gave him access to the castle, to Blaine, and ultimately gave him the opportunity to kill him."

Lady Diana sighed. "Now nobody will remember our anniversary party for the right reasons. This whole event has been a disaster."

A glimmer of irritation shone in Percy's eyes as he patted his wife's hand. "The most important thing is that the killer's been found."

Lady Diana looked away. "We'll have another party. And this time, we'll do a serious background check on any baker we employ."

"Holly could cater for you," Alice said. "I trust her one hundred percent, and she makes great cakes. I can guarantee she won't kill anyone."

"Thanks for that," I muttered.

Percy smiled at me. "You're welcome to cater for us any time, Holly. But I don't think we'll have another anniversary party."

"We will next year," Lady Diana said.

Percy glanced at her. "We'll talk about it later."

The kitchen door opened again. Campbell and Saracen marched in.

I jumped to my feet. "How did you know where I was?"

Campbell gestured for me to sit. "I know everything that goes on in this castle."

"You didn't know who the killer was," Alice said.

A faint flush crossed Campbell's cheeks. "We would have figured it out. Lila has been released, and the police are already questioning Lorcan."

I sat back in my seat. "But I didn't tell anyone about my concerns when it came to Lorcan. Did you have a bug in the bedroom? Was that how you knew where I was?"

"We don't bug the castle." Campbell glowered at me. "Fortunately for you, I hire the best. You brought in Saracen to run background checks on Lorcan, and he pieced it together. After you raced out of his apartment, he carried on looking at the evidence, alerted me, and we came to find you before you did anything foolish. I had to assume you'd blunder in and confront a killer with no backup. It wouldn't be the first time you'd done it."

Despite Campbell's insults, I smiled warmly at Saracen. "Thanks for saving me, Saracen. I definitely owe you for this."

He grinned. "I'll take my payment in all the date cookies you can bake. I'm just glad you're okay."

I blew out a breath and tipped my head back. "I live to fight another day."

"Until the next time," Campbell muttered.

"Let's take a break, Meatball." I'd made five cake deliveries this morning and was out of breath, my legs ached, and my lungs burned from all the exercise.

I cycled along the main street of Audley St. Mary and stopped outside my former café. I brought the bike up onto the curb and walked over to the window.

"Woof woof?" Meatball wagged his tail. He remembered this place. We'd spent so many happy hours here.

I lifted him out of the basket and set him on the ground to have a sniff around. "No, we can't go in. It's not ours, anymore. But it looks like it'll be opening soon." I stood and read the sign in the window.

Make your own arts and crafts. Grand opening in three weeks' time. We hope to see you here.

My bottom lip jutted out as I patted the window frame of the store. I couldn't deny the twinge of jealousy that somebody had taken it on. At least it was an independent store. When they opened their doors, I'd make them welcome. Maybe I'd bring them a cake. But I'd always think of this place as my café.

"Holly, just the lady I wanted to see."

I turned as Rupert climbed out the back of a black limousine. He wandered over, his hands in his pockets.

"Hi. I was just looking at my old café. I miss the place."

"So do I," Rupert said. "I could never resist the brownies you had on display. Though I'm glad you came to work at the castle."

"And brought my brownies with me. Every cloud and all that." I pulled my gaze away from the café. "Did you need something?"

"I absolutely do. I wanted to make sure everything was okay. How are you feeling after what happened with Lorcan?"

"I'm moving on," I said. "Everything feels like it's getting back to normal."

It had been two days since Lorcan had been arrested and charged with Blaine's murder. After denying everything for hours, he'd given in and admitted to what he'd done. It hadn't taken Campbell and the police long to discover the connection between the two men. They'd also interviewed witnesses who'd been at the party where Blaine had humiliated Lorcan, including Percy, and had confirmation of how badly Blaine had behaved.

I felt a degree of sympathy for Lorcan. Baking was such a personal thing; you put your heart and soul into making the perfect dessert. Criticism was always painful to take. It felt as if someone was attacking you when they didn't like what you made.

Rupert cleared his throat, drawing my attention to him. "I hope you don't mean literally moving on. I had a chat with Chef Heston about Lorcan trying to take you away from me. I mean, from the castle."

My eyebrows shot up. "Chef Heston doesn't care what I do. I'm surprised he told you about that."

"I caught him at a bad moment. He shouted at me, then realized what he'd done and was full of apologies. Of course, I didn't hold it against him, we all have off days. But I was interested to know what was wrong. He showed me the reference request Lorcan gave him."

"That put him in a bad mood?"

Rupert touched my arm. "Despite all the yelling, he values your work. Why else would he be so angry?"

I shrugged. I sort of knew that deep down. It would just be nice to hear it now and again.

"You were tempted to leave us?" Rupert asked.

My gaze ran over him. He was such a sweet guy, caring, kind, and clumsily funny. But he was also a complication I'd considered walking away from. "I did wonder about the offer. The glamorous lifestyle and trips around the world could have been fun. Sometimes you need to reinvent yourself and make changes."

"You only do that if you're not happy with your current life. You're not happy with us, Holly?"

"I … I'm happy." My gaze went to the limousine as the driver's side door opened. Campbell stepped out. He wore his sunglasses and his usual stern expression. He gave me a nod.

"You must stay. We have the ball coming up, the international history event, and that enormous wedding fair in a few months' time." He shuddered. "I need you around for moral support. I won't hear the end of it when the wedding fair is here. Everyone will keep trying to marry me off."

"Maybe you should think about getting married." I cast my glance his way. "Have you got anybody in mind?"

"I, well, gosh. I mean … it's a tricky business. A life partner, eh? I … I mean …"

I patted his arm. "Don't have a panic attack. I'm not making you a proposal. You don't rush these things. When you find the right person, you know. And speaking of marriages, you may like to speak to Percy. Things are tricky between him and Lady Diana."

"Oh! I wondered why they weren't talking. I'll suggest Alice speaks to them. I'm terrible at giving relationship advice."

"I think they'd appreciate some help," I said. "Things didn't look great between them when I saw them on the night of Lorcan's arrest. I hope they can resolve their differences."

"Of course. But you must stay, Holly. The castle won't be the same without you."

I smiled at him, my gaze going to Campbell, and then shifting to the top of Audley Castle in the distance. He was right. The place wouldn't be the same without me, but most importantly, I wouldn't be the same without all of this in my life. I loved living in the close-knit community of Audley St. Mary, surrounded by friends who I considered more like family, and the chance to bake to my heart's content.

"I'll beg if I have to," Rupert said. "I can't have you leaving us."

Meatball barked, bounced on his paws, and raced off along the street.

I made a move to chase after him, but Campbell grabbed Meatball and scooped him up before he got too far, before walking over to us. "Are you ready to return to the castle, Lord Rupert?"

"I am if Holly comes with us," Rupert said. "What do you say, shall we go back and enjoy some of your delicious cake?"

I smiled at them both as I petted Meatball's head. "Of course. Let's go home."

About Author

K.E. O'Connor (Karen) is a cozy mystery author living in the beautiful British countryside. She loves all things mystery, animals, and cake (these often feature in her books.)

When she's not writing about mysteries, murder, and treats, she volunteers at a local animal sanctuary, reads a ton of books, binge watches mystery series on TV, and dreams about living somewhere warmer.

To stay in touch with the fun, clean mysteries, where the killer always gets their just desserts:

Newsletter: www.subscribepage.com/cozymysteries
Website: www.keoconnor.com/writing
Facebook: www.facebook.com/keoconnorauthor

Also By

Enjoy the complete Holly Holmes cozy culinary mysteries
in paperback or e-book.

Cream Caramel and Murder
Chocolate Swirls and Murder
Vanilla Whip and Murder
Cherry Cream and Murder
Blueberry Blast and Murder
Mocha Cream and Murder
Lemon Drizzle and Murder
Maple Glaze and Murder
Mint Frosting and Murder

Read on for a peek at book four in the series - Cherry
Cream and Murder!

Chapter 1

"This makes a fun change from the bike, doesn't it, Meatball?" I glanced over from the driver's seat of the white van I drove.

"Woof, woof!" He wagged his stubby tail in complete agreement.

I grinned to see my fabulous corgi cross perched on my friend Louise Atkins' knee as we headed into Audley St. Mary to make a large delivery of cakes for a posh party.

"He's having a great time," Louise said. "And I can't wait to see this house. I've never been inside Marchwood Manor."

"Same here." I pulled the van to the side of the road to let a bus squeeze past. The roads around the village were mainly single lane, and I was used to racing about on my delivery bike, not driving one of the vans. But we had thirty trays of delicious treats to deliver to Sir Marchwood's party. They'd never have fit in the trolley I used to deliver cakes around the village.

Meatball bounced on Louise's knee and leaned forward, his pink tongue poking out. He was secured with a safety harness to the seatbelt Louise wore, so was perfectly safe.

"Holly, look!" Louise wrapped an arm around Meatball as she leaned forward in her seat. "They have unicorns at this party."

I slowed the van and squinted. Sure enough, there were two enormous creamy gray horses with elegantly styled horns strapped to their heads. I felt a bit sorry for them. I doubted the horses wanted to dress up for this event. They were magnificent enough without the fake horns and glitter on their skin.

I stopped the van by the entrance gate of the manor house. A large security guard walked over with a clipboard.

"Holly Holmes and Louise Atkins," I said. "We're delivering cakes for the party from Audley Castle."

He checked his clipboard before waving us through. The double gates opened in front of us, and I drove along the private road toward Marchwood Manor.

The manor house was almost as old as Audley Castle. It used to be owned by the Trevelan family, but was now looked after by Sir Richard Marchwood. He hadn't been here long, but was already known for his extravagant parties and VIP guest events. And it looked like he was adding unicorn themed parties to his social activities.

As happy as I was to be here and have a look around such a beautiful place, I really wanted to get back to the castle. We were hosting a huge event of our own, and one that was right up my street. It was a three-day history program and was just coming to an end. There had been fascinating talks, exhibits, and demonstrations of medieval weaponry.

I loved learning about the past. There was something so fascinating about how people used to live and how it shaped the way we did things today.

I parked in our allocated spot and climbed out of the van with Louise.

"You'd better stay here," I said to Meatball as he tried to sneak out the door. "You don't want to scare the unicorns. And Sir Richard may not like dogs."

"Woof." His little nose lowered.

I unwound the window and pulled a doggy treat from my pocket, which I handed to him. "You won't miss out on anything. And we won't be long. When we get back to the castle, I'll take you for a long walk this evening."

"Woof, woof." That earned me a small wag of his tail as he munched on his treat.

I walked around the back of the van, opened up, and started unloading the cakes onto the two trolleys we'd brought with us.

"Are those my party cakes?" Sir Richard strode out of the castle. He wore a green silk cravat under a pristine white shirt and black suit pants. He had a broad smile and a twinkle in his blue eyes.

"That's right, Sir Richard," I said. "Where would you like them?"

"In my hand. I always enjoy Audley Castle treats." He smiled at both of us. "Are you just delivering, or did you make these?"

"Holly makes the best treats in the castle," Louise said. "She's our baking genius."

"That's excellent news," Sir Richard said. "I insist on the best for my guests. I invited the Duke and Duchess to attend the party, but they told me they're hosting a history event."

I pushed the loaded trolley toward the manor house. "That's right. It's been a great event. We've had speakers from all over the country, including Professor Stephen Maguire. He's an expert in Tudor knights and medieval warfare."

"I've never heard of the chap. I always enjoyed English at school. That's what I studied at university." Sir Richard flipped open the lid of the top box and peered inside at the neat row of cherry cream tarts. "Mind if I try one?"

"They're all yours if you want them," I said.

"Don't tempt me. I have a terrible sweet tooth." He pulled out a glistening tart and took a bite. His eyes closed, and he groaned. "Absolutely delicious. My guests will be so pleased with these. Right this way. I'm at a loose end at the moment, so I'll show you through to the kitchens."

We made short work of unpacking the rest of the cakes, and after two trips to the van, the back was empty, only the faint smell of sweet pastry left behind.

"Before you go, here's something for your hard work." Sir Richard came out with two full glasses of what looked like champagne on a tray and two cherry cream tarts.

"That's very kind of you," I said, "but I'd better not have the bubbly. I'm driving."

"I'll have yours." Louise grabbed both glasses and took a sip. "This is delicious."

"And of course, you must have the tarts. Unless you get to overindulge in the kitchen and you're sick of your own baking." He passed us the tempting treats.

"There's always room for something sweet." I took both tarts, since Louise was busy downing the champagne like it was water. "I hope you enjoy your party."

"Thank you, my dear. I always do," Sir Richard said.

Louise made short work of the champagne before placing the empty glasses back on the tray. "Thanks. That was amazing. Even better than they serve at the castle."

"I won't tell the Duke that. He always claims he has the best wine cellar in the county." Sir Richard chortled before waving us goodbye as we climbed back in the van and drove away.

Louise hiccupped as she held the tarts and balanced Meatball on her knee. "How the other half live, eh? Think how much it must cost to heat a place like that."

"Probably almost as much as it does to heat Audley Castle," I said. "These old buildings are beautiful, but they take a lot of maintenance. I'm happy in my little apartment."

I had a small apartment in the grounds of the castle that came with the job. It had one bed, a tiny kitchen, bathroom, and lounge, but it was all I needed. Just Meatball and me, happy in our little piece of paradise.

"Shall we take a break?" Louise said. "We got unloaded quicker than I thought we would. Chef Heston won't expect us back for a while."

"Ten minutes won't hurt," I said. "And Meatball could do with a comfort break by the looks of things."

He was bouncing up and down on Louise's knee again, not paying the tarts any attention, and whining every time we passed a patch of grass. I knew the signs. He needed a toilet break.

I found a lay-by to pull into, close to a bench. I ran Meatball around the grass so he could do his business, then settled next to Louise, and we enjoyed our perfectly sweet and rich cherry cream tarts.

"Wouldn't you like a grand manor house to swan around in one day?" Louise asked.

"No. I'd be cleaning all the time and never get to enjoy it."

"You'd have staff to do that. And I hear Sir Richard is single if you want to marry into money." She waggled her eyebrows at me.

I grinned and shook my head. "You should have asked him out."

"Ha! Maybe I will. He seemed nice. A bit old for me, though. And it's a shame we only got to see the kitchen. I hoped we'd be able to poke about a bit."

"Give me a simple life over all the fanciness of a place like that." My life was good. I was happy in my job, Chef

Heston wasn't shouting at me all the time, I had Meatball, and great friends.

"By the time we get back, most of the history nerds will have gone," Louise said.

"Not yet. There's a final evening of lectures," I said. "It's an exclusive invitation only event. The Duke and Duchess arranged it for close friends and family, but I managed to sneak an invite from Princess Alice. And there's an archery contest tomorrow. That should be exciting."

"It doesn't sound all that exciting to me," Louise said. "Are we catering for the events?"

"Not tonight. But I'm making the desserts for the archery contest. I want to get there early to see people taking part. They'll be using replica longbows from medieval times. It'll be great."

She slid me a glance. "You have strange interests, Holly."

"There's nothing strange about liking history."

"What about dating? I don't see you doing much of that. Don't tell me you've given up on finding love and are only focused on stuffy history."

"Not exactly," I said. "But I already have the love of my life." I petted Meatball as he sat patiently, hoping we'd drop a few crumbs from our tarts.

"And he's a gorgeous little chap, but what about finding some delicious guy to spend your time with? I see you talking to Campbell a lot. He's yummy."

I wrinkled my nose. "I'm not interested in Campbell. Not as a boyfriend."

"He's often sneaking you off to have private chats. I think he likes you. I figured you were into him, too."

"No, he really doesn't like me. He's always telling me off. Besides, I like my men a little more geeky. You know, the bookish type. I want a man to seduce me with his brain, not his biceps."

"That's good to know," she said. "I'm tempted to ask Campbell out, but I didn't want to tread on your toes."

"Oh! Well, sure. You won't be doing that." I had a strange relationship with Campbell Milligan, the castle's head of security. Sometimes, we got along fine. Then we'd butt heads and our friendship would stall. Sometimes, it shifted into downright dislike.

"Do you know if he's dating anyone?"

"Um, he's never told me about a girlfriend. He's very private." I shrugged. "Don't you find him a bit scary? He has all those secret spy skills. What if you argued? He could make you disappear, and no one would find you."

"He's dangerous. I like that." She grinned at me. "You can guarantee you'd be protected if he took you out and you got in trouble."

"What kind of dates are you hoping he'll take you on that'll end in trouble?"

"The kind where I fall into his arms and he kisses me until I can't see straight. That's the sort of trouble I'm looking for."

I wrinkled my nose. "Campbell doesn't have a romantic bone in his body."

"I hope he's not into adventurous things that involve being outdoors." Louise's mouth twisted to the side. "I won't enjoy that. I should invite him to dinner. We could have a romantic candlelit dinner for two, and I could see if there's a soft side to Campbell."

"I've never seen one," I said. "Come on, we need to get back to the castle."

The three of us climbed back in the van. I'd only driven a short way along the road when the steering wheel tugged to the left.

I stopped as we reached the junction. "Take a look at the passenger side wheel. I'm having difficulty steering."

Louise wound down the window. "Uh oh. We've got a flat tire."

I grimaced as I pulled the van to the side of the road. We got out again and peered at the flat.

"Do you know how to change a tire?" Louise asked.

"Sure. So long as we've got the right equipment." I went to the back of the van and opened up the footwell. There was a jack, a lug wrench, and a spare tire.

I frowned as I checked the tire. It was also flat. "We have a small problem."

"No tire?"

"No air in the tire," I said.

"We'll have to ring for a rescue service."

I turned as a vehicle pulled up alongside us. It was a familiar black land cruiser used by the security teams at Audley Castle.

One window slid down, and Campbell peered out. "What are you doing here?"

I sighed. Trust him to find me when I'd gotten in difficulty. "Just dealing with the small matter of a flat tire."

A smile tracked across his face. "Don't tell me you've broken the van?"

"No! It's simply a flat. It could have happened to anyone. And I've just discovered the spare is useless. Is there any chance you can give us a tow back to the castle?"

"There's zero chance of that. Hold on. I'll sort this." Campbell reversed his vehicle behind ours. He climbed out, accompanied by two other security guards, Mason Sloane and Kace Delaney.

"It's my dream come true," Louise whispered in my ear. "We were just talking about him, and here he is. Should I ask him out now?"

"Maybe not right now," I said. "Campbell likes to compartmentalize. He has a single-track focus when he's working."

"He can have a single-track focus on me anytime he likes."

I glanced at Louise and shook my head.

Campbell walked around to the front wheel and kicked it gently. "It's flat."

"Didn't I just tell you that?" I said.

He checked over the spare tire. "This is flat as well."

I resisted the urge to tut. "Have you got something we can patch it up with?"

"Sure. Mason, get the repair kit from the trunk."

Mason nodded and headed around the back of the vehicle before returning with the repair kit.

"This is a temporary fix," Campbell said. "Don't drive any long distances or it won't hold. And when you drive back to the castle, stay below thirty miles an hour."

"That won't be a problem around here," I said.

Campbell took off his jacket and rolled up his sleeves before setting to work on repairing the tire.

"You look like you work out," Louise said.

I glanced at her and raised my eyebrows. Was she really going there, even after my warning?

"I need to keep in shape for the job," Campbell said, his attention on the tire.

"I need to get fit," Louise said. "Maybe you can give me a few pointers. Do you think I have a good figure?"

He grunted. "Holly works out a lot. Ask her. She's always trying out some weird fitness trend."

"My interest in fitness isn't weird," I said.

"You do like unusual things," Louise said. "Didn't I hear about you doing yoga with goats?"

"That was fun," I said. "And Princess Alice organized that for me."

"I'm sure you've got a few fitness tricks you can show me," Louise said to Campbell. "I'm a fast learner."

"I'm happy to hear it." He stood and nodded at the tire. "That's good to go. Mason, switch over the tires for these ladies, and we can be on our way."

"On it, boss." Mason disappeared around the side of the van with Kace.

"Thanks for helping two damsels in distress." Louise fluttered her lashes at Campbell. "We'd have been stuck if you hadn't come along."

"I'm sure we'd have figured out something," I said. "You were talking about calling for a tow truck just before Campbell arrived."

"There's no need for that," Campbell said. "This was an easy fix."

"I couldn't have done it. You're so clever," Louise said.

Campbell glanced at her, and his eyes narrowed a fraction. His attention flicked to me. "I've seen you around the history talks."

"I couldn't keep away. It was so interesting. I loved the presentation on etiquette in the royal household. And the demonstration of ancient weapons was mind blowing." I glanced at Louise. She was frowning. "Louise also likes history."

Campbell tilted his head at her. "You do?"

"Oh! Um, I mean, sure." She looked at me like I'd been speaking another language. "Why not? All those weapons and... things. Do you like history, Campbell?"

"It's not my thing."

Her shoulders slumped. Campbell wasn't making this easy on her. Louise was pretty, fun, and making it very clear she was interested in him. He wasn't picking up the hints.

"Did you see the display of weapons?" I asked. "They were authentic, discovered during several archeological digs. The lecturer said they're making replicas to test."

"It sounds riveting," Louise said, not looking at all interested as she kept staring at Campbell.

"I prefer a modern gun," Campbell said. "You don't get automatic firing and a fast reload with those ancient hunks of metal."

Of course, he would say that. "Did you hear any of the talks? The debate on the construction techniques of Kings College Chapel was interesting."

"You're being a geek," Louise whispered.

Campbell smirked. "I'll be glad when they all clear out. The extra people around means double shifts for my security team."

"Most of them will be gone by the end of the night," I said. "Then you can get back to standing around outside the family's private rooms, trying not to look bored."

"Holly!" Louise slapped my arm. "Campbell and his team do an important job protecting our employers."

Campbell grinned. "That's right. My job is crucial. Thank you for noticing."

Louise giggled. "You're most welcome."

Ugh! This was getting embarrassing. "Will you be at the shooting contest tomorrow?" I asked Campbell.

"I'll be there. Princess Alice and Lord Rupert will be attending, so security will be on hand if needed."

"You should take part in the contest," Louise said. "I bet you'd win first place."

"I would, but it's only fair to give the other contestants a chance," Campbell said.

I groaned as his huge ego made an appearance, while Louise sighed and batted her eyelashes again.

"I'm planning on getting there early to watch the action," I said. "And I've created a menu of Tudor and medieval treats for the participants to try."

"And I'll be there, too," Louise said. "You need an extra pair of hands on the day, don't you Holly?"

"I guess so. You're welcome to come along." Her offer wasn't motivated by a desire to help me. She wanted more time with Campbell.

But the man appeared immune to her flirting. His back was straight and his hands clasped behind him. Maybe he did have someone special in his life. For all I knew, he could have a secret wife tucked away.

"All finished," Mason said as he strolled back around the van with Kace.

"We'll see you back at the castle. Drive carefully." Campbell nodded and headed back to the vehicle with his colleagues before they drove away.

"He's so gorgeous." Louise climbed back in her seat and settled Meatball on her knee. "You'll have to put in a good word for me."

"Campbell never listens to anything I say." I pulled out and headed to the castle.

"You could at least find out if he's single," she said. "I don't want to waste my time chasing after a man who's not available."

"I'll see what I can do," I said. "But no promises. Whenever I ask Campbell questions, he gets mean."

Louise sighed and fanned her face with a hand.

I shook my head and laughed. My thoughts briefly turned to Lord Rupert Audley. Now, he was my type. I could go for a guy like that. It was just that, I couldn't go there with him. We were friends, and I was fine with that situation. Although, sometimes, I did wonder, what would life be like being involved with Rupert?

I rolled my shoulders and concentrated on the road. I already had everything I needed to be happy. A great job, friends, and my favorite little dog by my side. I couldn't want for anything more.

Cherry Cream and Murder is available to buy in paperback or e-book format.
ISBN: 978-1-9163573-3-4

Here's one more treat. Enjoy this delicious recipe for mouth-watering vanilla cake. Duchess Audley approved!

Recipe – Mouth-watering Vanilla Cake

Prep time: 20 minutes **Cook time:** 1hr 20 mins

Stays fresh for 3 days, or in the freezer for a month.

Recipe can be made dairy and egg-free. Substitute milk and yogurt for a plant/nut alternative, use dairy-free spread, and mix 3 tbsp flaxseed with 1 tbsp water to create one flax 'egg' as a binding agent (this recipe requires 12 tbsp flaxseed to substitute the 4 eggs.)

INGREDIENTS
1 cup (227g) unsalted butter, softened
1 cup (227g) golden caster sugar
1 tsp vanilla paste
4 large eggs
2/3 cup (85g) plain flour
1/2 cup (113g) full-fat Greek yogurt
1 cup (227g) self-raising flour
3 tbsp milk
For the syrup (store bought is fine. I love Sweet Freedom.) Or make your own with 1/4 cup (50g) caster sugar and ½ tsp vanilla paste

INSTRUCTIONS

1. Heat oven to 160C/140C fan. Grease a round, deep 20cm tin, then line with non-stick baking paper.

2. Beat the butter, sugar, vanilla, and ¼ tsp salt until pale and fluffy, then pour in eggs, one at a time, giving the mix a beating before adding the next egg.

3. Beat in the yogurt. Mix the flours and fold into the batter, followed by the milk.

4. Spoon the mix into the tin and bake for 1hr 20mins or until risen and golden.

5. Make the syrup by heating 50ml water with the sugar and vanilla in a pan until the sugar dissolves. Set aside. Once the cake is cooked, leave to cool for 20 mins, then use a skewer to poke holes in the cake. Pour the syrup over, letting it soak in.

Cook's tip: Delicious with a top layer of ready roll icing.

Cook's tip two: Store bought vanilla syrup works well.

Made in the USA
Coppell, TX
11 August 2022

81310079R00135